It all began
over a steer.

A puncher found the steer one day up on the range where the Chaney and Morgan interests overlapped. The Morgans said the steer was theirs. The Chaneys said it belonged to them.

Then a couple of the Morgan boys tried to settle the argument with guns.

The Chaneys retaliated with a raid that killed three men.

Finally, there was an all-out battle, and when it was over, fifteen men lay dead. Everybody in town knew that more were going to die.

That's when Barry Litton rode into Holy Creek and decided to put an end to the bloodshed by taking the law into his own hands!

Books by Max Brand

Ambush at Torture Canyon
The Bandit of the Black Hills
Black Jack
Blood on the Trail
The Border Kid
Danger Trail
Destry Rides Again
The False Rider
Fightin' Fool
Fighting Four
Flaming Irons
Ghost Rider
   (Original title: Clung)
The Gun Tamer
Harrigan
Hired Guns
Larramee's Ranch
The Longhorn Feud
The Long, Long Trail
On the Trail of Four

The Outlaw of Buffalo Flat
The Phantom Spy
Ride the Wild Trail
Rippon Rides Double
Rustlers of Beacon Creek
Seven Trails
Singing Guns
Steve Train's Ordeal
The Stingaree
The Stolen Stallion
The Streak
The Tenderfoot
Thunder Moon
Tragedy Trail
Trouble Kid
The Untamed
Valley of the
   Vanishing Men
Valley Thieves
Vengeance Trail

Published by POCKET BOOKS

THE LONGHORN FEUD

•

Max Brand

A KANGAROO BOOK
PUBLISHED BY POCKET BOOKS NEW YORK

THE LONGHORN FEUD

Dodd, Mead edition published 1933

POCKET BOOK edition published August, 1948

3rd printing......................March, 1977

This POCKET BOOK edition includes every word contained in
the original, higher-priced edition. It is printed from brand-
new plates made from completely reset, clear, easy-to-read type.
POCKET BOOK editions are published by
POCKET BOOKS,
a Simon & Schuster Division of
GULF & WESTERN CORPORATION
1230 Avenue of the Americas,
New York, N.Y. 10020.
Trademarks registered in the United States
and other countries.

ISBN: 0-671-81267-X.

Cover illustration by John Leone

Printed in the U.S.A.

CONTENTS

THE LONGHORN
FEUD

1. DRINKS ON A STRANGER

EVERY ONE IN HOLY CREEK REMEMBERS THE DAY THAT Barry Litton, better known as Blue Barry, came to town, because most of the people had a chance to see him, and to see him in action, before that day ended.

It was during the hot middle of the morning—though any time after sunrise was hot in Holy Creek—that a man on a mule rode into the place, following a tall fellow on a mare, brown with black points. They were dust-covered. There was nothing distinguished about them, except the dainty way in which the mare picked up her feet, and the width between her eyes, and the smallness of a muzzle fit to drink out of a pint pot, as the Arabs say of their chosen horses.

When the two came to Pudge Oliver's saloon, they rode in under the wide roof that was built out as far as the watering troughs. Under that roof Pudge Oliver always kept the sand well wetted down with buckets of water, and although that water was apt to be steaming at the edges, where the sun got at it, it looked cool and inviting to any one who was thirsty, and it drew a great deal of patronage into the saloon.

The tall man drew rein, and looked over a line of idlers on the veranda. They were resting between drinks, and exchanging gossip.

"Willow!" he said.

The man on the mule tumbled out of his saddle, and ran up to salute the first speaker. "Yes, sir?" said he.

The idlers on the veranda looked at one another, and sat forward. Citizens in the town of Holy Creek were not addressed as "sir" unless they were very old indeed, and very much respected.

They were the more surprised because Willow himself wore an air of importance. He was not very tall, but he had a ponderous torso mounted on a pair of bowed legs that looked made to order for hooking around the sides of a rambunctious horse. Furthermore, as he saluted, the loose sleeve of his coat fell back a little and showed a wonderfully brawny forearm covered with hair, and through the shadow of the hair gleamed the reds and purples of some elaborate tattooing.

Here was a man who seemed to have been through the wars; the sort of a man who might have been picked to boss a round-up, and yet he was "sirring" his companion.

"Willow," said the first rider, "this looks like a place where a fellow might have a drink, eh?"

"It's kind of got that look, sir," said Willow, cocking his eye at the battered swinging doors that admitted one to the sanctum. He licked his dusty, cracking lips as he spoke.

"You can't tell by the outside of a place, though," said the tall young man. "Go inside and have a look around, will you? If it seems real on the inside, come out and tell me, will you?"

"Sure I will," said Willow, and proceeded to do so.

He went hastily up the steps and through the swinging doors.

Of course this was at the time when the great Chaney-Morgan cattle war was on—the war that began over the steer that finally had a death's head branded into its side, so that it was called the Dead Man Steer. And it just happened that Jerry Deacon, of the Morgan outfit, was in that saloon at the time, having a drink and a little argument with a stranger over the merits of the case. Since the stranger disagreed, at the very instant that Willow pushed the doors open, both men were going for their guns, and Jerry Deacon was a split second faster than the other fellow. His bullet laid the other's forearm open to the elbow. The stranger dropped his gun, and stood stupidly looking at the running blood.

"Hey, quit messing up the floor!" shouted Pudge Oliver. "Go into the back room, there, and let the cook tie you up."

Willow stepped outside the swinging doors and hailed his companion.

"It looks real and it sounds real," he said.

"That doesn't mean anything," said the man on the mare.

So Willow reëntered, and at the bar ordered a drink. He paid for it, sniffed it, and drank it.

He went back to the swinging doors and opened them a second time. "Smells real and tastes real," said he.

"Every man can make mistakes," said the other. "Have another drink."

Jerry Deacon's blood was up. He had meant to split the wishbone of yonder stranger, and he was grieved and surprised because his bullet had travelled a whole three inches outside of his intentions.

He said, "What tastes real, and what looks real?"

"The whisky and the blood," said Willow, ordering another drink, and licking his cracked lips. "But I got a boss that's hard to convince. Have a drink with me, bo?"

There were two things about this speech that were offensive to Jerry Deacon. One was that he was called "bo," which as all people know is short for "hobo," and the second was that any one should dare to speak lightly of his gunwork.

He edged closer to the bar, as he answered, "I don't drink with strangers."

"Stay dry, then," remarked Willow, as he rolled the second glassful over his huge tongue.

"I dunno that I'll stay dry, either," said Jerry Deacon.

"Go and be damned, then, if that suits you better!" said Willow.

"Is that your game?" remarked Jerry Deacon. And dropping the weight of his stalwart six feet and three inches behind the blow, he hammered a straight right against the chin of the stranger.

Willow went backwards on his heels, taking both short steps and long. He hit the doors with his shoulders, stumbled backwards onto the veranda, and nearly fell.

"And it *is* real," he shouted to his friend. With that he charged back into the saloon to renew the battle, because he, too, was a fighting man.

The tall fellow now slipped from the brown mare and entered the saloon at the rear of the crowd which was pouring in to see the fight. And as they livened the air with their cowboy yells, he saw Willow receive a right and a left, a beautiful one-two punch, flush upon the end of the chin.

Again Willow staggered backwards on his heels. He

11

should have fallen in a crumpling heap, except that he was made of iron.

After him came big Jerry Deacon. Jerry was good with a gun, but he was far better with his hands. And now he wanted nothing but to smash the stranger to bits. He might have done it with ease, because Willow's hands were down and his eyes were bleared. It was not kindliness that prevented Deacon from doing just that; but as he charged he was tripped from the side, and almost fell on his face.

This was interference. It was almost mockery. Deacon forgot all about the half-beaten form of Willow, and whirled about, yelling, "Who did that?"

"I did, brother," said Willow's friend. "He's five inches shorter and thirty pounds lighter than you are."

"I'll lighter you!" cried Jerry Deacon. He was half minded to draw a gun and work in blood, as he said this, but the stranger stood with his hands on his hips, and with such a peculiarly mocking smile on his lips that it seemed to Jerry there would be no satisfaction in anything except in a laying on of hands.

So he went in to break the stranger up, but he did not go in blindly. A really good boxer never does that, and Jerry Deacon was really good. He came with a beautiful long left that worked with oiled precision, though it carried all his weight.

Somehow he missed the mark. He lurched forward, his impetus spent on the thin air; and then the floor rose with dizzy suddenness against the face of Jerry Deacon, and at the same instant the ceiling dropped upon his head. His brain was covered by a wave of utter blackness.

It had all been very quiet and simple, but keen eyes had been watching. Men who rope steers and pitch hay understand that strength is nothing and art is everything. So they comprehended that twitch of the shoulder and that lilt of the body which had cracked a hundred-and-eighty pound whiplash neatly on the chin of the redoubtable Jerry Deacon.

Two or three men ran forward to help the fallen man, but the stranger remarked, "You'd better leave him there. If his neck's broken, you can't do him any good. If it's not broken, he needs some time to cool off before he comes to. Step up and liquor with me, boys, because this looks to me like a real town, full of real people."

He smiled on them and laughed with them as he said this. And suddenly Jerry Deacon was forgotten. He lay there bleeding quietly on the floor, gradually recovering his wits, while the others filled their glasses from the bottles that Pudge Oliver spun up and down the length of the bar, bringing them to rest at the appointed intervals.

Pudge Oliver filled his glass with the rest, invited by a cheery nod from the stranger. "What's your name, brother?" demanded Pudge.

"My name is Barry Litton," said the stranger.

"Blue Barry is what they call him," said Willow. "Blue for the color of his eyes."

"Here's to you, Blue!" called the saloon keeper. "Here's in your eye!"

"Here's in everybody's eye!" said the stranger. "May the world never be rounder!"

They turned bottoms up, and Willow said to a neighbor, "Anybody know that gent on the floor?"

"I know him," said the man addressed.

"He's good with his fists," said Willow, "but he's had enough from that side of the page. Maybe when he wakes up, he'll start dreamin' about guns. If you know him, you better try to lead him out of here on the quiet. Because if he starts any more trouble, that poison will start workin' on him—under the skin." He hooked a significant thumb towards Barry Litton, as he spoke.

The cowpuncher who had been thus addressed, after a glance at Litton, went to the place where Jerry Deacon was just beginning to bestir himself on the floor. What's the cowboy said to Deacon no one could hear, but it was enough to make Jerry Deacon arise quietly and slip almost unnoticed from the saloon, one hand pressed thoughtfully against the bump that was rising on his jaw.

2. WHERE THEY GROW WILD

PUDGE OLIVER WAS AS HONEST AS HE WAS FAT.

"Litton—or Blue—or whatever they call you, mostly," he said, "you may have worked up a neat little bit of trouble for yourself."

"How come?" asked the tall young man, with his cheerful smile.

"Why," said Pudge Oliver, "it's this way: Jerry Deacon is one of the best men that the Morgan bunch have got, and they're likely to chip in on his side. You wanta watch you step, unless there's some Chaneys around. They'd take mighty kindly to anybody that had socked Jerry on the chin the way that you've just gone and done!"

"What's eating the Morgans and the Chaneys?" asked Blue Barry Litton.

"It's a steer," said Pudge.

"Can't the steer eat hay, and not men?" said Litton.

"It's this way," explained the bartender, while the rest of the crowd listened with interest, though to them it was a familiar tale. "It's this way. There was a steer, d'ye mind, up on the range where the Chaney and the Morgan interests sort of overlapped. A Chaney puncher brings him to the round-up with the right earmark; and there's a Morgan man at the round-up, and he points out that the second part of that earmark is pretty doggone fresh, and without that second part of the earmark it would be a real Morgan steer. Pretty soon those two boys get out their guns and shoot themselves sick. But the Chaneys, they get the steer, in the wind-up; and then the Morgans come over, and by night they cut the steer out of the night herd of the Chaneys, on Chaney ground, and take it back and put it up in their corral. The Chaneys get real wild when they hear this. They get a bunch together, and they make a morning raid, like old Injun days. There's three men killed in that party—two Chaneys and a Morgan, because the Morgans were ready and waiting, and they turned the Chaneys back . . .

"A while later, the Chaneys try again, and this time they get the steer, but they don't go far, because the Morgans overtake 'em. There's a fine battle, and out of fifteen men there ain't a one that ain't sick with the lead that's in him, before the finish. The steer runs loose. A coupla times the Chaneys catch him up, and the Morgans come shootin' for him. A coupla times the Morgans catch him up, and the Chaneys start up the war again; until finally the sheriff takes and catches up that steer himself. Somebody'd branded the critter with a death's head above a pair of crossed bones.

"The sheriff's got the steer now, holdin' it in the name of the law, till a lawsuit is decided on the ownership. Because the Chaneys got the first law decision, and the Morgans, they won the case on appeal; and now it's in a higher court. They say that the sheriff will sell that steer, if anybody's willing to buy it, because he's tired of feeding it. But, first and last, fifteen men have died for that Dead Man Steer, and more are gonna die, before the end."

"Why doesn't the sheriff knock the steer on the head?" said Barry Litton.

"Why, he don't dare to," answered the bartender. "And nobody else would dare to, 'less he wanted both the gangs down on his head. The time has come, around here, when there ain't nothing but guns and gunmen, and the days are pretty bad."

"Why," said Litton, "seems to me you're selling your share of whisky."

"Sure I am," answered Pudge Oliver, "but there's been so many holes put in the walls and the roof of this here place by bullets which missed the mark, that when the rains commence she's gonna leak like a sieve. I've lost seven of them big mirrors from behind the bar; an' finally I give up, and kept that cracked one. Most men can't stand the pace here in Holy Creek—and doggone me, neither can the glassware!" He sighed as he said this.

"That's a good name," remarked Barry Litton. "That's as good a name as I ever heard for a town—except that it takes a little for the saying of it."

"It's this way," said one of the punchers near Blue

15

Barry. "In the old days there was a Mormon or something comes by this way, and he takes and breaks a wagon here, and has to stay awhile—with all his wives and children. It happens that while he's here there's some rains, and a little water is runnin' in the draw, outside of town. So he calls it Holy Creek, and puts up a sign to that effect when he goes on. But there ain't any Creek, really, and it sure ain't a holy town. Still, I guess that's why the name has stuck so good!"

There was more laughter, after this recital.

"It sounds to me," said Barry Litton, "like a really good place for a man to put up."

"It is," declared Pudge Oliver. "The whisky keeps well here, as long as it's in the barrel. It's that kind of a climate. You take a lot of places, there ain't any regular wind that blows in the middle of the summer. But here in Holy Creek there's wind pretty nearly every day in the year; just like a dragon was breathing in your face."

"It sounds pretty good to me," said Barry Litton.

"People here don't use starch when they wash clothes," said Pudge, "and that's a saving."

"Why no starch?" asked Barry Litton.

"Because the salt of a gent's sweat will stiffen his shirt for him in a coupla hours, any day," said Pudge Oliver.

"I like this kind of town," said Barry Litton, "because of the people that are in it. It takes a cool man to live in as hot a town as this. Why did you choose this place, brother, to put up a saloon?"

"I've been run out of all the other counties in the state," said Pudge Oliver. "That's one reason. And the other reason is that the folks around here are afraid to drink the water. The whisky's purer."

"I think I'll try my luck here," said Barry Litton.

"What kind of luck do you like?" asked the bartender, while the others listened more intently than before.

"I like," said Barry, "four crooks all sitting at a table with a lot of money in their wallets, and asking for a fifth hand. That's the sort of weather that I bloom in."

They laughed again, as they heard this.

"How about a common or garden greenhorn—a regular tenderfoot with a million in his bank?" asked Pudge Oliver. "You wouldn't shy at that kind of a mark, would you?"

"I don't like that kind," said Litton. "Green fruit always makes me sick. I never eat it. The harder the nut, the sweeter the kernel, brother."

He produced three dice from nowhere, threw them to the ceiling, and made them come rattling back into his palm. "That's the music that I like to hear," said he. "But I don't like the boys to think that they're playing against luck when they're playing with me."

"Look here," said Pudge, "you mean to say that you make a living out of the cards and the dice? Without keeping your game on the quiet?"

"It's this way," answered the stranger. "The more I talk about it, the more some of the wise ones will wink to themselves. They know that a really handy man with the cards never boasts. And they can't help asking me to sit down while they trim me. That's the way I always make my stakes. Right now there's some of the boys along your bar that would like to ask me to a little card game.—Speak up, brothers, and lemme know the truth!" He looked up and down the line.

A long, lean-faced man with an eye that was the blue-gray of steel, looked back up the bar and said, "I'll play with you, son. I'll see how good you are!"

"It's a match!" called several others.

But Blue Barry cheerfully answered, "No, you're a working man. You can't juggle the cards or make the dice talk back to you unless your hands are soft. There's a pair of hands, gentlemen, that are always kept soft. Look at them! The pride of my life are those hands. Never done a stroke of work in their lives—and they never *will* do a stroke of work, until I change my mind!"

He spread his hands on the bar. Brown, beautifully tapering, slender and long, they looked almost like the hands of a woman; but they were big, with muscular cushions under the thumbs.

"Does it pay you, brother?" asked the bartender.

"Why, man," answered Litton, "what d'you think—I've been around the world, and lived on the fat. I walk where I want to walk, and I talk where I want to talk. I've done so much for these hands of mine that they wouldn't lie down on me and give me a bad deal in return."

"Well, then," said Pudge Oliver, "what brings you out

17

here? If you've got what you want other places, why would you want to come here?"

"That's easy," said Litton. "It's partly because it's in my blood. But more than that, it's to fill out my game."

"Well?" asked Pudge Oliver.

"There's plenty of money in the rest of the world," said the stranger, "but there's a shortage of men. A big shortage, mind you! I came out here where they grow wild. I want to see what they're like!"

3. A DRINK ON THE SHERIFF

THEY WENT OUT INTO THE SUNSHINE, LITTON AND Willow.

"Still like this port, Tom?" asked Litton.

"I never like it much, even when I first heard you speak of it," said Willow. "I only said it was real. And you ain't asked what part is real about this harbor."

"Well, what part, then?"

"The reefs and the sunken rocks," said Tom Willow. "They're the *real* part of it, sir."

"We'll make it like home," declared Blue Barry. "With a good navigator like me, Tom, and a good hand like you at the helm, we'll be right at home. Where does the sheriff live, I wonder?"

"Sheriff?" exclaimed Willow. "What on earth do you want with a sheriff?"

"I want to see the steer he's boarding," said Litton.

"I knew it when I seen your face!" said Tom Willow. "When I seen you shining your eyes, I knew that you had ideas, and all of my bones, they begun to ache all at once—and all over."

"Why, what's the matter, Tom?" asked Litton.

"Aw, I dunno," said Willow. "I guess I'm gettin' old. Ridin' fifty miles a day, that ain't nothing. Crossin' a few deserts is nothing but fun. A few sand storms—what

18

are they to talk about? As for livin' on what we can shoot, in the way of skinny rabbits and what not, I guess that kind of chuck is too good for an old tar pike me. And as for a few slams on the jaw like I got from Jerry Deacon, who must have had sledgehammers tucked into his hands, why, they're just enough to make the fun right. So I dunno why it was that I got sort of an ache all over when I seen that light in your eyes.—Only, I guess I'm gettin' old. I've seen a lot of lightning in the sky, sir; but when I see yours, I always know that it's gonna strike—and that it's gonna strike right near me!"

He ended this speech with a sigh, and a shake of the head.

"He hit you pretty hard," agreed Litton. "I've tried to teach you how to use your head for ducking and riding with punches, instead of using it like a wall for the other fellow to break his fists on. You've never learned the trick, though."

"It's this way," said Tom Willow. "A fight is a fight, and I dunno that I ever minded a good, straight fight. But my idea of a scrap is where you slug and get slugged, and the one that slugs the hardest, he wins. But I never held by these here stampings and dancings, and all of that. They kind of upset me, and I ain't at home with 'em. But if it was a fight where you rough-house, then I'm kind of easy, because that's the way I was raised. It ain't everybody that has a chunk of lead pipe on the end of a string, the way you have when you sock a gent on the chin, sir."

The other shrugged his shoulders. "If you can't remember anything else," Barry said, "remember that crouch, and the long left. Anyway, Jerry Deacon got just a little more than he sent."

"He was cock-eyed," said Tom Willow, with a grin of delight. "He certainly was knocked for a loop." He chuckled.

"About this town," said the master. "I'm sorry you don't like it. Because to me it looks like a bright place."

"Yeah—and I knew you'd like it," agreed Tom Willow. "A place where they even brand their cows with a death's head. You couldn't help liking that kind of a joint."

Willow paused, and then added, "Trouble is the stuff for you to breathe, all right—except the kind that comes too far south."

"What do you mean by that?" asked Litton.

"South Seas," said Tom Willow.

"Why," said Litton, "that's the cream of the world, Tom!"

"Ay," nodded Willow, "but I've seen the cream turn sour. When you saw Stacey—"

He held the next words back by clicking his teeth together, and stared with frightened eyes at his companion. Blue Barry had halted in mid stride. Some of the color left his face. He looked straight before him, out of narrowed eyes, as though he was confronting a levelled gun.

"I'm sorry," said Willow. "That damned name—it just sort of slipped out!"

"That's all right," said Litton, drawing a deep breath and walking on. "It's a jolt when I hear—Well, let it go."

They went on in silence, Tom Willow still watching his master with eyes of fear and awe.

Litton hailed a freckle-faced youngster who was passing, scuffing his feet for the sole purpose of raising a vast cloud of dust.

For his own part, the boy did not mind dust; as for others, the more he could annoy them, the more he admired the effects.

"Where's the sheriff to be found, partner?" asked Litton.

The boy shrugged one shoulder. "Somewhere between here and a bad time for somebody or other," said he. He walked on.

The long arm of Litton went out and collared him. The boy turned, a green light in his eyes.

"Leave me be!" he said.

"Where do I find the sheriff?" asked Litton.

"Leave me be!" said the boy, "or I'll punch you in the stomach, you long-legged chunk of nothing-worth-while. Leave me go!"

"I told you it was a good town, Tom," said Litton. "Even the boys have learned how to talk, eh?—Listen, partner," he added to the boy, "I like to wring necks, but I don't want to start on you unless I have to. Where does the sheriff live?"

"In his house," said the lad.

"That's news for me," remarked Litton. "He lives in his house, an' not in a hotel, eh?"

"There ain't any hotel," said the boy. "Leave me go, or I'll break your shins!"

"You've told me everything that I want to know," said Litton. "The sheriff lives in his house down the street."

The eyes of the boy glinted again. "That's right," he said, "down the street."

Litton turned him loose. "He lives *up* the street," said Barry. "That's all I can find out. I tell you what, Tom, this town gets better and better! This is the sort of a town that I call *hard*."

"I could of told you that a long time ago," said Willow.

They turned back up the street, and after walking some distance, Litton stopped in front of a house with a short, high veranda before it. A long-haired, gray-bearded man sat in a rocking chair on the porch, smoking a pipe with a curved stem.

"Morning," said Litton. "Can you tell me where the sheriff's house is?"

"What's the trouble?" said the man with the pipe, speaking from a corner of his wide mouth.

"No trouble.—I just want to find the sheriff."

"Nobody wants to find the sheriff," said the gray-beard, "unless there's trouble. What's the matter with you?"

"It's about the steer that the sheriff keeps."

"Oh, is it?—And you mean to say that steer ain't trouble?"

"It's no trouble of yours," broke in Tom Willow.

"What makes you think it ain't?" asked the man on the porch. He now developed sufficient interest to cause him to remove the pipe from his mouth. When that was done, he looked calmly down on them. "That steer's a whole pile of trouble to me, I can tell you."

"Can you tell us where we can find it, then?"

"In the back yard."

"What back yard?" asked Litton.

"The sheriff's back yard."

"That puts me back at the beginning," said Litton. "I want to know where the sheriff lives."

"What sort of trouble are you in?" repeated the gray-beard.

"Damn it all!" said Litton. "I'm *not* in trouble. Whose backyard is that steer in?"

"In the sheriff's back yard, like I told you," said the man on the porch.

They seemed to have reached a complete impasse. The man on the porch replaced his pipe between his teeth and looked calmly and vaguely across the roofs of the other houses, towards the blue mountains. It was plain that he considered the conversation at an end.

"Hold on," said Litton, taking up a new thread. "How does it happen that that steer gives *you* trouble?"

"What steer?" mumbled the other.

"The Dead Man Steer."

"Because I have to take care of it," said the man on the front veranda.

"Oh, you work for the sheriff, do you?"

"No."

"Who *do* you work for?"

"Myself," said the veteran.

Litton began to chuckle. "You've got me puzzled," said he.

"You ain't the first," said the other.

"Who are you?" said Litton.

"The oldest man in Holy Creek," said the man on the porch.

"I believe it," said Litton. "You're the oldest man—and you're the toughest."

"Young feller," said the man of the beard, "if you get fresh, I'll come down there and put my hands on you."

"All right," said Litton. "I can't find out who you are, and I can't find out what you do, except that you take care of the steer, and that you don't work for the sheriff."

"That's right," said the other. "Now you boys trot along and leave me to my smoke."

"But the sheriff has to take care of the steer," said Litton.

"Never said he didn't," replied the other.

"Then you're the sheriff?" asked Litton.

"You can make up your mind for yourself," said the other.

"Why, now I come to look again," said Litton, "I've seen pictures of you."

"It's the long hair that makes them take pictures of me," said the other. "Every damn fool who sees my long hair says that he's seeing the real wild and woolly West, and he gets out his camera. I've busted twenty-thirty cameras in my time. I hope I'll last to break twenty or thirty more."

"You're the famous sheriff," said Litton. "You're Sheriff Dick Wilson."

"I never said I wasn't," said the other.

Litton walked up the steps and shook hands.

"I'm Barry Litton," said he.

"Never heard of you," answered the gruff sheriff.

"No," said Litton, "but you're going to."

At this, Dick Wilson took his pipe from between his teeth and looked the visitor up and down. "What do you want around here?" he asked.

"I want the steer," said Litton.

"What you want it for?"

"Because I haven't had any pets for a long time," said Litton. "I need something to play around the room and lie down on my feet to keep 'em warm of a cold evening. I need something with an eye that will brighten when it hears my footfall. I need something on which I can lavish the love, Sheriff Wilson, which is man's inherent gift from the Creator, and which man must give again, sir—be it on high or low—else the spirit which—"

"Why," interrupted the sheriff, "doggone my hide if you don't talk like one of these here damned sky-pilots!"

"Thank you very much," said Litton.

"I didn't mean it for a compliment, neither," said the sheriff.

"Oh, I know," said Litton, "you're one of those diamonds in the rough—one of the hearts of gold under a rude exterior—one of God's Gentlemen—"

"Hey, quit that, will you?" said the sheriff, in haste.

"I'm just trying to be agreeable," remarked Litton.

"You ain't, though," said the sheriff. "I don't agree with nothing that you say!—I'd like to know something, though. Where'd you come from?"

"From right over there," answered Litton, with a wave

of his hand that included half of the points of the compass.

"I thought you did," replied the sheriff. "The big wind come from the same place, too. Don't give you no pain to keep on talkin' the way you do?"

"Not if I can get the Dead Man Steer," said Litton.

"What would you do with it—aside from makin' a parlor pet out of that longhorn?"

"Why," said Litton, "I'd simply teach it to do a few tricks, and then I'd put it in a pen and charge five cents a head for a look."

"You wouldn't make much money," said the sheriff, "because there ain't many people in this town, an' most of 'em has seen the steer, one time or another."

"The boys would come in from the range to look."

The sheriff arose with a sigh. "I wouldn't wanta try to talk you down," he said, "because I see that you thrive on talk. If you want that damn' steer, you know what you'll do?"

"Yes, I'll keep it behind a fence."

"Until the Chaneys or the Morgans decide to come down and take it away from you. Come on and see the damn' thing, though."

He led the way to the rear of the house; and there, in a small corral close to the barn, stood a big longhorn. It was fat and strong, with sleepy eyes; it chewed its cud. In the full blaze of the sun, it was a yellow-gray in color, with a yellow spot over one eye and a black spot over the other, which gave it an odd effect of looking in two directions at the same time.

"That's the steer," said the sheriff. "I gotta hold it till the lawsuit's settled. But law ain't ever gonna settle that. Blood's the only thing that'll ever lay the dust."

"Well," said Barry, "I'll take that steer off your hands, and I'll produce it when you want it."

"Take it then," answered the sheriff. "That fool steer can eat up five dollars' worth of hay in a week—unless you put green glasses on it and feed it sawdust for grass."

"Hey, Dick!" called a raucous voice from the other side of the high board fence of the corral.

"Yeah?" asked the sheriff. "Whacha want, eh?"

"They's been a rumpus down at Pudge Oliver's place."

"Anybody dead?"

24

"No, but a limber lookin' gent come to town and got arguin' with Jerry Deacon. Knocked Jerry cold."

"Nobody is knockin' Jerry Deacon cold," said the sheriff, "except with the butt of a gun, or a club."

"This gent done it with his fist. I seen him. He's got a bow-legged sailor along with him that started the fight; but the young bird was the one that finished it—whango! You better come along down and be on deck, because the whole doggone Morgan clan is pretty sure to come pilin' into town lookin' for that man."

"Go back and tell the boys that the stranger is by name of Litton, and that I've hired him to keep the murder steer for me. That'll cheer things up around this town, a pretty good deal."

There was a yell of surprise from the man beyond the fence, and then a scurry of retreating footfalls.

The sheriff grinned broadly. "Looks to me," he said, "like this town was gonna open both its eyes, pretty soon. Looks to me like I feel younger than I did a while back."

"Good," said Litton. "Willow, bring a rope, and we'll take that little steer away to his new home."

Willow brought the rope. The yellow steer, trained by much handling in the course of his life, came on the lead as readily as a dog. With his eyes half closed, and still chewing his cud, he ambled down the street behind Willow.

"Which way?" said Willow.

"The hotel," said his master. He screened his eyes, for he was looking against the sun. He stared fixedly at the great brand which had been drawn with a running iron on the flank of the steer. Whoever had made it was an artist, for it was an excellent representation of a human skull and a pair of crossed bones. As the skin of the steer's flank stretched and puckered with the steps he was making, the skull seemed to grin and scowl.

"How does it look to you?" asked the sheriff.

"It looks like a lot of fun for me," said the other. "So long, sheriff."

"Hold on," said the sheriff. "I got a brand of whisky in the house that needs to be tasted. Come along in and try a swig of it."

They entered the house, where the sheriff did honor to his roof by pushing his hat on the back of his head. The stranger removed his entirely.

Now the sheriff indicated a great ten-gallon jug that stood in a corner. "Here's a glass," he said, giving one to Litton. "Now just help yourself, Mr. Litton. Go just as far as you like."

Litton did not hesitate. It was a ponderous stone jug, and it was brimming with liquid. Yet he did not put the glass on the table and use both hands to manipulate the great container, for he understood perfectly that the sheriff was quietly attempting to discover what amount of muscle was stored in the arm that had knocked down Jerry Deacon. Sheer effort would hardly manage the thing, and he knew that, also. Any human wrist would snap under the strain of lifting the great jug and turning it sidewise. But Barry Litton picked up the jug, gave it an easy, pendulous swing, and then quickly shifted it so that the bulky jug lay within the crook of his arm. He drew the cork.

The hardest effort of all had to be made in order to pour the liquid out into the glass in a steady stream. His whole arm and his shoulder ached with suppressed shudders as he strained to accomplish this. But he managed it. Without a tremor, a small amber stream poured out until two fingers of liquor lay in the glass.

Still he persisted in keeping the jug under his arm. "Have some yourself?" he asked.

"Sure," said the sheriff, his eyes glistening. He held out his glass and into it fell the same slender, steady stream.

The test was not over, however. The sheriff's glass was given back to him, and after that young Mr. Litton had to swing the jug down from his arm without breaking his wrist—and place it on the floor without a jolt. He accomplished that trick.

Last of all, he had to hold the glass in his strained right hand, and drink it without letting a tremor show. This he could not do. Speed would have to cover that weakness; and so saying, "Here's in your eye, sheriff," he nodded to his host, scooped his own glass from the edge of the table with a swift gesture, tossed off the liquor, and immediately replaced an empty glass on the table.

The sheriff looked on with greater pleasure than ever. "Muscle—*and* brains," he said. "Good luck to you and the Dead Man Steer, brother!" Then he drank his own portion of the dregs.

4. SIGNS OF THE TIMES

YOUNG MR. LITTON OVERTOOK WILLOW JUST AS THE latter was approaching the neighborhood of Pudge Oliver's place.

He said, "Tom, the time has come for us to settle down for a little while."

"Sure, I knew that, I knew that," answered Willow. "We'll settle down here in a harbor full of reefs open to the wind, with a steer called the Dead Man for an anchor to windward. Ain't that the plan?"

"That's the advantage of having had you with me so long, Willow," said Litton. "You know what's in my mind —and that's a great thing for me."

"Me?" said Willow. "I don't know what's in your mind, and I don't wanta know. I ain't such a fool that I wanta *know* the future. I'd rather keep *hopin'* about it."

"The first thing," said Litton, "is to get a place to stay here in town—somewhere on the edge of it. Next, we'll have to put in a supply of guns, because we may need some of 'em, Willow. You can see that. The people around here have an itch that only a spray of lead can cure."

Willow groaned, but made no answer.

"You collect the horses," directed Litton, "and I'll step into the gun shop and see what they have in the way of what we want."

"Samuel Raeburn, Guns and Ammunition," was the legend that appeared above the door of the shop.

Pushing open the door, Litton stepped in and found

sitting on the counter the same freckle-faced lad whom he had collared on the street, not long before. The boy's hands were idly gripping the edge of the counter, and his brown, bare legs were swinging. He looked at Litton with blank eyes.

"You the proprietor of the shop, brother?" asked Litton.

The boy's bland, deceptively innocent expression did not change as he called out, "Hey, Lou!"

A girl's voice answered, "Yes, Jimmy?"

"Come and look at," said Jimmy.

Footsteps hurried, a door was pulled open. "That worthless mongrel of yours has treed my cat again," scolded the girl in the doorway. "If you—" She paused, seeing the stranger. With eyes as blue and bright as Blue Barry Litton's eyes she looked straight back at him.

"Look at," said the boy. "This is what I wanted you to see.—This is the one that grabbed me on the street."

"I want to look at a pair of eight-bore double-barreled shotguns," said Litton to the girl, "and a couple of Winchesters."

"Yeah," said Jimmy, "I knew you'd be needing guns, pretty soon. Maybe you'll be needing a grave before long."

The girl had laid the guns on the counter in silence. But now she said, "Jim, get off that counter and go away! You're rude."

"Him and me are both rude," admitted Jimmy. "But he's the rudest. He's the one that licked Jerry Deacon, down at Pudge Oliver's."

"Jimmy, get out of the store!" exclaimed the girl.

"She's none too pleased about Jerry getting a sock on the chin," explained the boy, slipping from the counter and going towards the door, though at a snail's pace. "She's pretty crazy about Jerry.—That big ham!"

His sister gave him a calmly disdainful glance.

"Here are the Winchesters," said she. "They're all the same, and all good. These shotguns are right, too," she added.

"How do you know?"

"I've used the same kind myself," said she.

He looked at the heavy guns, and then at her slenderness.

28

"She's pretty proud of that," said Jimmy. "She puts in about that every time she can."

A side flick of the eyes touched Jimmy, but failed to daunt him. Still he moved towards the door, and still his progress was that of a snail.

"These will do," said Litton. "I'm sure the shotguns are all right. But the rifles? Well, I'll have to try one of 'em."

She filled the magazine without a word. He felt a certain curiosity behind her eyes, but saw that she would not let it rise to the surface.

And he, thanking her, stepped to the door. "Come along, Jimmy," he said, "and show me something to shoot at."

He saw a slight movement on the part of Lou, as though she longed to be present at that testing, but he left her uninvited.

Jimmy, aggressively eager, hurried forward to open the door. In the blaze of the sun before the shop he stood beside the tall man, glancing hungrily around him.

"There!" he said.

"Where?" asked Litton.

"See that sign?—That sign that says 'Morgan and Company, Grain, Hay, and Livestock,' right there across the street?"

"Well," said Litton. "What about it? There's another sign just opposite that says 'Chaney and Company, Grain, Hay, and Livestock.' Which shall it be?"

"Take either one of 'em," said the boy. "They're hangin' by a pair of wires each. If you can shoot those wires in two, it proves that the rifle carries pretty straight, doesn't it?"

"And the signs fall?" suggested Litton, grinning.

"That doesn't make any difference," said Jimmy. "The Chaneys and the Morgans are dead pleased when anybody shoots down those signs. It gives them a lot of free advertising."

"Well," said Litton, "why not? You know, Jimmy, the way I'm fixed in this town, it won't do for me to let people think that I'm a bad shot. Because I'm not. I'm pretty good."

"Oh, are you?" said Jimmy, sneering instantly at the first suggestion of bragging.

"I'm not a champion, but I'm pretty good," said the other. "And it's only fair to let people know it."

Jimmy, with an uncertain mind, stared at the big man. Then he shrugged his shoulders, reserving judgment.

Litton, in the meantime, looked earnestly at the gleam of the heavy wires that upheld the Morgan sign. Then he lifted the rifle quickly to his shoulder.

The butt had hardly settled into the hollow of his shoulder before he pulled the trigger. The great sign swung down and hung by a single wire.

"Jumping jiminy!" said Jimmy, under his breath. He looked up with worshiping eyes at the stranger; and, behold, as the sign swung slowly back and forth, the rifle spoke again, and the heavy board crashed to the ground.

Jimmy yelled with joy.

From the great, yawning double doors of the warehouse ran two or three men. They recoiled with shouts when they saw the figure with levelled rifle across the street. But the direction of the weapon was no longer towards them.

"If the Morgans are down," said Litton, "turn and turn about is fair play. What about the Chaneys?"

Straightway the rifle barked twice, and the Chaney sign smote also the dust and broke in two.

Jimmy could no longer shout. His eyes were two blue and white saucers. And Litton, turning, had a faint glimpse of a girl's face, pressed so close against the front window of the store that the nose made a white spot on the pane.

He reentered the door as Lou Raeburn was scampering to regain her place behind the counter. She was panting a little, and her eyes were dancing as he paid his bill.

"Straightest shooting rifle I ever had," said Barry Litton. "Maybe I can get some advice, here?"

"You bet you can get advice," said Jimmy, his voice a crow of ecstasy.

"I want to find a shack on the edge of town—a place to rent. A couple of rooms would do. Know about a place like that?"

"Si Turner's place," said the boy and the girl, in one breath.

"Will you show me, Jim?" he asked.

"Don't forget about ammunition," said Jimmy. "Oh, but there's gonna be a stir. The Chaneys *and* the Morgans! Both slapped in the face! Wow!" The boy who liked to kick up dust yelled with joy.

So it was that ammunition in quantity was bought.

"Have you got a lot of friends?" asked the girl behind the counter.

"Quite a few, here and there," said Litton, who was standing at the door.

"You'd better spend the night writing to them," said she. "They'd probably all like to have a farewell letter!"

"I might do that," he answered, "but I haven't any writing paper with my crest on it." He passed out to the street, with Jimmy fairly dancing beside him.

Already a crowd was gathering around the fallen signs, and more men and women and children were coming at full speed.

"You've raised a dust, all right," said the boy. "Look at 'em! By jingo, won't the Chaneys and the Morgans choke!"

Tom Willow, with the two horses and the steer, stood near by.

"Great thunder, sir," said he. "What you been up to?"

"I was trying out a rifle," said Litton. "Which way is the Si Turner place?" he asked of the boy.

"Right down the street, between them two fallen signs," said Jimmy.

"Go down the street," said Litton to Willow, "and we'll overtake you. Where's there a shop to buy chuck, Jimmy?"

"There's Mayberry's, across the way," said Jimmy. "They've got everything from whole sides of beef to crackers."

"We'll try Mayberry's," said Litton.

They crossed the street, and as they crossed, Litton called after Willow, "Step up and give Chaney and Morgan enough money to pay for putting their signs back in place, will you, Willow?"

There was a groan from that worthy, and Litton and the boy entered Mayberry's big store.

"Look," said Jimmy, "there's everything that anybody could want, here."

31

"Go on and order, Jim," said his companion.

"Me? Me order?" exclaimed Jimmy.

"That's the idea. You order. Nobody knows what he wants to eat, after he gets past twelve or thirteen years old. But at that age a fellow knows exactly what he wants."

"You like jam?" asked Jimmy, wistfully. "I mean, with bread that's *thick* with butter?"

"Nothing better, now that you speak of it," said Litton.

"And sardines?" asked Jimmy.

"Yes, and sardines, of course! You go ahead and order."

"How much?"

"Why, as much as you think a pair of people would want to have around them, if they were staying a month or so."

Jimmy's blue eyes flared with joy.

He stepped to the counter. "Hey, you," he said to the clerk.

"Whacha want, Jim?" asked a yawning clerk.

"Trot out that deer that was brought in this morning."

"How much of it?" asked the clerk.

"The all of it," said Jimmy. "There's gonna be venison ate around this town, before long.—And rake down that shelf of blackberry jam. I wish that there was two shelves, but I'll take what you got.—And all the canned brownbread that's in the place, too."

"Hey, Jim, what sort of a jamboree is this going to be?" asked the clerk. "And who's gonna pay for this here?"

"This here gentleman is gonna pay for it all," said Jimmy. "I wantcha to know, boy, that a gent has struck Holy Creek who knows what *chuck* is!"

5. WITHOUT WARNING

LITTON AND THE BOY LEFT THE STORE, AND TOGETHER they went down the street.

"You coming to Turner's place with me?" Litton asked.

"Say," said Jimmy, "what are *you* doing with the Dead Man Steer?"

"I'm keeping it for the sheriff," said Litton.

"What for?"

"I'm going to charge nickels to the boys who want to see it—except you, Jim. You're in on the ground floor."

"Nickels, eh?" questioned Jimmy. "How about bullets?" Will they do? Because you're likely to get a whole flock more of them than nickels."

"I'll take whatever I can get," answered Litton. "Mind you, partner, if you walk down the street with me now, you're liable to collect a bullet or two your ownself."

"If they can hit me, they can murder jackrabbits on the run," boasted Jimmy. "Come along!"

So they sauntered down the middle of the street.

"It makes dusty walking, here in the middle of the street," said the boy.

"It does," answered the other, "but it gives you a chance to look at the doorways behind you."

They drew near the crowd that now spilled quite across the street from the Chaney to the Morgan warehouse. And as they approached, an avenue opened up before them.

Jimmy, delighted, could not help thrusting out his chest like a pouter pigeon.

"Something's gonna break now," he said.

"Not yet," answered Litton. "They'll need a little time to make up their minds. Anyway, we'll see how hard this town is."

"It's plenty hard," said Jimmy.

33

They had come to a spot midway between the two stores when a gray-headed man, big and walking with long strides, came out to them. He pointed a finger at Litton.

"You're the man who shot down that Morgan sign?" he asked.

"I am," said Litton. "I needed to try out a rifle I'd just bought, and I thought if I paid for the damage—" He was smiling gently as he spoke.

"You and your damages be damned!" said the big man. "This ain't the last you'll hear of shootin' down signs in Holy Creek!"

"Brother," said Litton, "I'm moving into the Si Turner shack, and if anybody wants me, I'll be found there at regular hours—and irregular hours, too. The Dead Man Steer will be at home there, too. Five cents is all I charge."

He drew himself up. Then, looking deliberately to the right and the left, over the heads of the others, he remarked, "But it doesn't look as though I'll collect much money in this crowd."

"Doesn't it?" demanded the other. "What do you—"

"It doesn't," said Barry Litton, "because it doesn't look to me as though there are many men in the lot of you who are *worth* a nickel!"

With that he strode on, leaving behind him the men who had been drinking in the scene, their eyes and ears dumfounded.

Jimmy scurried at the side of his long-stepping companion. "Jumping jiminy!" said he. "You know who that was?"

"The gray-headed fellow? No."

"That was Rush Morgan himself, and he's the head of the whole clan," said the boy.

"Is he?" said the other carelessly. "I'm glad I've seen him, then."

"But look here!" said the boy. "If you—" He paused, unable to speak more, and looked at the load of guns carried over the bend in his companion's left arm.

Then he shook his head. "What brought you out here, partner?" said Jimmy filled with a deep awe and even deeper worship.

"Why," said the other, "a friend of a friend of mine

wrote about Holy Creek. I thought since I was travelling this way I might as well look it up."

"Who was it that wrote?"

"A man called Pete. Red Pete. Red Pete Chalmers was his name."

"Red Pete?" asked the boy. "Why I know about him!"

"Do you?" said Litton, with seeming carelessness.

"They bumped him off."

"Why, who killed him?" asked Litton. "Was he a bad actor?"

"He wasn't doing nothing," said the boy, "but he got in between, when the Morgans and the Chaneys met up, one time, right here in town. It happened right back there. They opened up, and he got in between. He was the only man killed that day."

"Wouldn't the fool move when they yelled to him to get out of the way?" asked Litton even more carelessly. But his face, which was turned a trifle away from the boy, had turned a shade pale under the tan. His jaw was set like stone.

"There wasn't anybody shouting to him to get out of the way," said the boy. "They just opened up and blazed away at each other, and he happened to be in between."

"Yeah?" murmured Barry Litton. "Was it a Morgan or a Chaney who got him?"

"Nobody could tell," said the boy. "He was right in between. It might have been either of the lot, or both."

"Kind of hard luck for Red Pete, eh?" said Barry Litton, laughing.

There was a hard grating sound in the laughter. The boy did not notice it, however. He looked up with amazement at a man who could be so totally callous.

"Yeah, it was hard luck," said the boy. "Kind of mean luck, too," he continued, "because, like you say, you'd think that people would give a sign to folks in between, before they start in shooting."

"Yes, a fellow would think that," said Litton. "Still, I don't know. A man has to take his chances."

"Yeah. But there weren't no chances—not for Red Pete. It made me sick when I seen him spin around and drop."

"Oh, you saw it, did you?" said Litton, with an imperceptible start.

"It was close to the shop, you see," explained the boy, "and I was there near the window. I looked out and saw the shooting begin, and I saw Red Pete grab his guns as he fell."

"He went for his guns, did he?" asked the other in a faint voice.

"You bet. He had a gun in each hand as he hit the dust, but he hit the dust dead."

"That was his bad luck," said Litton.

"He was a fine big gent, too," said the boy. "He was your size, partner."

"Was he?" murmured Litton. His voice was almost inaudible.

"And he had eyes about like yours—mighty blue," said Jimmy.

"Yeah?" drawled Litton. He gave a sudden shrug to his shoulders, as though a chill had run down his spine.

"Say—he was a ringer for you," said the boy, "except that he had red hair.—I never thought of that before!"

"Yeah, I guess a lot of people look like one another," remarked Barry Litton carelessly.

"But not ringers—like him for you," said the boy. "They got him planted out in Boot Hill, and nobody but half a dozen would know where the grave is."

"Why," said Litton, "some day we might step out and take a look at it—just for curiosity, eh?"

6. MRS. MURDER

SI TURNER'S PLACE LAY ON A SLIGHT RISE OF GROUND at the end of the village, and on the way to the shack they routed out Turner himself to conduct them to the old house. He was living in a new one, now—a tall, narrow house with two stories and an attic, the attic being Si Turner's chief pride. Whenever he made a lucky strike in the hills and sold out his claim for a comfortable sum, the very first thing that he thought about was a house with an attic; for, as he explained to young Barry Litton, a one-story house was all right for a young fellow, but by the time a man had accumulated a past he needed some place to put it.

"There's my old traps, for instance," said Si Turner. "Why, some of them old bear traps of mine have got a history behind them. I tell you what, I can read inches deep in the rust; they are covered with fine print for me, brother.—Then you take things like old broken snow-shoes, they walk me right back through times that give me a chill up the back, I can tell you. And where's there a place for 'em except in an attic? No, sir, I tell you what—a house without an attic is like a man without a memory."

The old shanty which Barry Litton had asked about was composed of two rooms, a kitchen-dining room and a bedroom-parlor. There was a stove in the kitchen; there were two bunks built against the walls of the other room. There were a few other articles of furniture, about which Si Turner made the comment, "They don't look right, sitting around the new house; and they're too good to store in the attic. So there's a good many times when I come up here and spend an hour or two fiddling around the old house, thinkin' things over.—You take and look at that 'M. W.,' carved into the side of that table, good and deep. It was carved by a good deep kind of a man. Them initials was sunk there into my table by Milton West. It wouldn't be hard to prove to my grandchildren, if I ever got married and had any, that Milt West was a partner of mine. There's things about Milt and his fights and his travels that would make a man keep on thinkin' for an hour at a time . . .

"There's other things about the house that might be you'd like to know about. There's that slice above the door. Maybe you wouldn't know that Tom O'Shay, he put that cut there with his own hand? Yes, sir, the ax he throwed didn't hit me, but it took the hat off my head and jammed it into the wall, there. Look close an' you can see some of the threads that still stick there in the crack.—You see?"

"I see," said Litton.

Said Si Turner: "It never would hardly be possible

37

for me to be lonesome, up here in this shack.—There's that cobweb, d'you mind?" He pointed to a great sheet of silver silk that filled an upper corner of the ceiling.

"That's a big cobweb," said Litton. "That would be good for stopping a flow of blood."

"Well, maybe it would," said Si Turner. "I reckon that anything cobwebs would be good for, that one would be extra fine at. Well, I've seen that cobweb made and kept for eight years, partner! Yes, sir. For eight whole years she's hung there. And the old lady spider down there in the sack at the corner of the web, with her hands stretched out on her telegraph lines, waiting for news of raw meat. There's many and many a time, I can tell you, that I've sat here, of a summer afternoon, and caught flies and hoisted them up and dropped them on the web, and watched old Mrs. Murder come bustling out and grab the fly. I've listened to his poor wings sing for a second or two; and many a morning I've looked down in the corner and seen the dead, dry bodies that Mrs. Murder had heaved out of her house!

"There was a day when I seen a big hornet go whang into that nest, and bust about half of the main cables at one crash. Out comes Mrs. Murder on the run. I aimed to think that she'd cut the hornet loose before he spoiled the rest of her web; but not her. She begun to throw out films of thread, and pretty soon she got one of those wings of the hornet nailed down. He was still thrashin' around and tearin' things up; and finally, all that web was down except where the ruins was hanging by the ends of two or three of the main cables. It was a sad thing to see that fine old web danglin' around in the wind that the hornet kept up with his one wing.

"But by jiminy, I tell you what—Mrs. Murder, she kept at her work, and finally she got the other wing lashed; and then she went down, mighty careful. I stood on a chair and watched that hornet gnashing his teeth and sticking out his sting, like the head of a spear, and all shining with poison. A coupla times it looked to me like he was gonna put an end to Mrs. Murder; but at the last she got him, and what was left of that fella is back in my attic, glued to a bit of card. There ain't more'n a shell left to him, and yet you can't hardly see where that old lady put in the knife!—No, sir, I never seen a better spider than her; a more keener spider, or a neater about her housework—or a brighter, or a more entertaining spider. For a long winter evening, I wouldn't know whether I'd rather spend time with old Milt West, when he was alive, or watching that spider up there. Why, she knows me, doggone her!"

He tapped the web with a straw, and out ran a long-legged, hairy horror of a spider, to pause in the very center of the web.

"There she is!—There's Mrs. Murder for you," said old Si Turner. "Ain't she a beauty?"

"She's as good a spider as I ever saw!" declared Litton, with a slight shiver in his shoulders.

"You give her a fly or two, now and then," said Si Turner, "and the first thing you know, you won't be reading your paper, of an afternoon.—You'll be cocking an eye up at that web."

Si Turner pointed out other objects of interest on his place. He had been faced with the great question—Ought he to take electricity into the house, or not? But electricity finally had come in; and as Si Turner said, it made the house as bright as day!

This house, with all of its carved initials, its electric light, corral, shed, and spider webs, was for rent at the small figure of ten dollars a month. Barry Litton paid a month in advance. Then Si Turner shook hands, wished him luck, and wandered back down the road.

Jimmy, in the meantime, had scouted about the place and delighted himself with all that was in it.

"Here comes the grocery wagon, loaded down," said Litton. "You tell the driver where to put the stuff in here—if there's room for it in the kitchen. I've got to go out and have a talk with Tom Willow."

"Partner," said Jimmy, "I'll have everything stowed away like in a pack—with a diamond hitch throwed onto it!"

Tom Willow had put the mule and the horse in the shed in the meantime; and the corral was left to the wanderings of the Dead Man Steer. It was a good corral, with a muddy little stream of water trickling across one corner of it, and a fresh growth of grass covering the ground. The Dead Man Steer began to graze in the most peaceful manner, while Barry, his new guardian, looked down upon him with thoughtful interest.

Both the Morgans and the Chaneys had been slapped in the face on this day; and now the steer was virtually a red rag that would flap in their faces. Barry Litton was more and more pleased as he considered this matter.

From among the many boxes sent up from the grocery store he selected the smooth, pinewood sides of two, and upon these he wrote in large letters:

T R E S P A S S E R S   B E W A R E ! ! ! ! ! !

Underneath, he wrote in smaller letters:

ANY ONE ENCROACHING UPON THIS GROUND WITH-OUT PERMISSION DOES SO AT HIS OWN RISK.

Barry turned to Jimmy, who had just finished storing and stacking the provisions in the kitchen. "Hey, Jim!" he said, "come here a minute, I've got an errand in town for you."

"Yeah?" said Jimmy, dimly, speaking around a mouthful of fig cookies that distended his jaws grotesquely.

"Will you run down to the sheriff and ask him if he has any objections to my shooting trespassers after I've put out these signs?"

"Hey," murmured Jimmy, "you wouldn't mean to be really shooting a fellow that just happened along, would you?"

"Go along, Jim, and do what I ask," Barry said. "Take the mare, if you want to, and she'll have you there and back in two jumps. I'm going to lie down and take a nap."

"Are you going to sleep, just when all the excitement's commencing?" asked Jimmy, amazed.

"Yes," said young Barry Litton. "I sleep better when I'm thinking, and I think better when I'm asleep."

Jimmy Raeburn started, cogitated for a moment, and suspected that a joke might be hidden behind those words. But he got the mare, saddled her, shortened the stirrups to suit him, and mounted.

She pitched him, straightway, up onto the slanting roof of the shed, and from this height he rolled off and fell to the ground. A grown man would have been hurt badly, but Jimmy was half wildcat and half boy, so that he landed on hands, knees, and feet. Presently he arose, hardly hurt.

A voice called from the kitchen door, "Come here, Nance!"

The mare, with a fling of her head, one ear forward and one ear back, came dubiously to her master.

"Come here, Jimmy," said the master.

The boy approached.

"Here, Nance," said Litton, "I want you to meet my old friend Jimmy. Shake hands with him, girl.—That's better. That's the way to be friends.—Jimmy, this is Nance. Give her your hand. Now she'll be all right. Climb right on."

Jimmy climbed on, not at all sure of himself. But the mare, after fidgeting for a moment or two, went off gently enough at his mild urging. It still seemed to Jimmy, however, that her bright eye was rolled back at her master, as he stood watching from the kitchen door.

The boy gathered courage and tried her at a trot—and to his amazement, he hardly stirred in the saddle. He tried her at a gallop, and the mare's long, bounding canter lifted the boy's heart into his throat with wings. Tears of pleasure stung his eyes. *This* was the life! And yet for all the might in her stride, Jimmy found that as soon as he grew accustomed to the rhythm, he could sit her without the slightest trouble. Every instant he seemed to fit into the saddle more and more firmly, more tender on the bridle, and observed her fine ears pricking. She seemed to be looking off towards the horizon, as though that far blue region was the ground she longed to gallop over!

Jimmy stopped at the door of his father's shop.

"Hey, Lou!" he called.

His sister opened the door. "What're you doing on that horse, Jimmy?" she asked.

"Me and Barry Litton are partners," said he. "I'm gonna spend a lot of time up there at his place."

"Are you?" said she. "Is he shooting down any more signs?—Showing off, I call it."

"You're mad because he licked Jerry," answered Jimmy. "So long, Lou. One of these days I'll give you a ride on the mare, maybe."

There were still a few people in front of the two warehouses. The Chaney sign was being repaired; the Morgan sign still remained upon the ground. And as the boy rode past, he saw grown men turn their heads and watch him with wonder as he shot past on the horse that belonged to the formidable stranger.

The boy found the sheriff sitting on his front porch, as before. "Hey, Sheriff Dick!" he called.

"Hello, you young hoss thief," said the sheriff, speaking around the stem of his huge pipe.

"Suppose," said the boy, "suppose a gent puts up a sign that says nobody can come onto this place, then somebody comes onto it. Suppose he shoots them, is it all right?"

The sheriff took the pipe from his mouth and thought over the words. "That's kind of a fine point in the law," said he. "I dunno about it. Maybe he'd better shoot a couple first, and then see."

"Yeah. But he wants to know," said the boy.

"It's kind of a fine point," repeated the sheriff. "What would he be wantin' to shoot people for, if they come onto his place? How many would he go and shoot?"

"He don't care," said Jimmy. "It don't make no difference to him who he shoots."

"Maybe not," said the sheriff. "The difference is mostly to them that get shot. I dunno but he's gotta right to shoot the gents that walk in on him. I wouldn't be shooting too many right at the start, though. Folks need a while to get used to new ideas, like that."

"He can shoot 'em, then, can he?" snapped the boy.

"I reckon he could shoot a few. You tell him he'd better put a notice in the paper first, though. That would make it all right. You put a thing in the paper, and then it's legal to do anything you want."

When Jimmy reached the Turner place again, he tiptoed to the doors, and found his new friend lying face downward on a bunk, soundly sleeping.

Jimmy put up the mare and saved his news, going out to the corral, where Tom Willow was busily stringing a quantity of barbed wire around the outside of the fence.

"What's that for?" asked the boy.

"How would I know?" said Willow. "It's orders, is all I know."

"Look," said the boy. "How you come to hook up with Blue Barry?"

"It wasn't my fault," said the other. He stopped his work, leaned on the top of a corral post, and began to fill an old black pipe with old black tobacco, wet and heavy with molasses. "I was in a port, once," said he.

"Where?" asked the boy.

"A long ways south," said the other. "I was aimin' to enjoy myself, and I was sort of likkered up, when a lot of doggone yellow Malay niggers took out to keel-haul me. They come with knives to do it. I got into a corner and fought, but a table hit me from somewheres, and I dropped. The next I knew, I was being lifted up by the nape of the neck, and I was getting my eyes open to see a young gent before me with the clothes mostly tore off his back. The room was a wreck, and there was blood, here and there. And off in the distance there was howling and yelling for the dead . . .

" 'Who are you?' says the young gent before me. 'I'm Tom Willow,' says I, 'on shore leave from—'

" 'You come with me,' says he, 'and never mind your shore leave. You'll get your shore leave from me after this.'

"So I looked into the blue eyes of him, and I knew that I'd found my master at last. When he said to come, I went—I've been going ever since."

7. A REAL PARTY

WHEN SAM RAEBURN WALKED OUT TO THE SI TURNER place that evening he found four signs at the four corners of the little field in which the house stood.

Halting, he shook his head. Then he called loudly, "Jimmy! Hey, Jimmy!"

"Yeah?" shrilled a voice.

"Come here!"

"Whacha want?" shrilled the voice of the unseen Jimmy.

"I want you!"

"What for?"

"Jimmy, come here!"

"I'm comin'."

The front door of the shack opened, and Jimmy's face appeared.

"We're just gonna have supper," he said. "You never seen such a spread."

"You come on home," said Raeburn.

Blue Barry appeared in the door behind Jimmy. "Come in, Mr. Raeburn," said he.

Mr. Raeburn came and looked at the food that was heaped upon the table. He discovered two kinds of bread, three sorts of cakes, nuts, raisins, figs, delicious cakes of dates, to say nothing of oranges, apples, and other things arranged in a veritable mound in the center of the table. At this same moment perspiring Tom Willow jerked open the door of the oven, and a savory cloud of steam from a venison roast exuded into the room.

"Why," said Mr. Raeburn, "it's quite a spread you boys are having."

"Spread?" said his son, enraged and desperate at this understatement. "Why, it's Thanksgiving and Christmas and Hallowe'en and New Year's and Fourth of July and everything all rolled in together."

"Sit down, sit down, Mr. Raeburn," said Blue Barry, "and have a slice of roast venison."

"Why," said Raeburn, "if you're insisting, I could take a taste and still have an appetite left for supper, I suppose."

"Keep your hands off of that oven door!" roared Tom Willow, suddenly. "I'll make a derelict of the first gent that lays his tarry hands on that there oven door. That venison ain't done, and nobody this side of hell is gonna lay a tooth onto it before it's done. You hear me talk?"

This thunder made Mr. Raeburn start. He glanced towards Blue Barry Litton; but the latter, though a frown of protest was on his forehead, merely shrugged his shoulders.

"When Tom's cook, he's the cook," said Litton. "And

there's very little that I can do about it. Sit down here, sir, and try some of his tobacco in your pipe."

Mr. Raeburn was charmed. One did not meet such cordial hospitality every day. Besides, he felt it an honor to be the only member of the community who was permitted to enter the house. After all, he would only stay a moment—and what was five minutes?

Besides, his young son stood at his shoulder, giving his arm a covert squeeze and whispering, "Gee whiz, pop! Ain't he wonderful? Look at him—that's Blue Barry!"

Willow began to compound a gravy. The fragrance of it filled the very soul of Samuel Raeburn.

Time fled. The outer sky was darkening. The window pane was a solid block of black into which sank the reflections from the room.

The further to enchant the flying moments, young Mr. Litton had some pleasant remarks to make about Jimmy that made Jimmy burn with pleasure, and even made the face of his father flush. It appeared that Litton could not possibly have succeeded in anything, from the moment he arrived in the town, had it not been for Jimmy's help. Mr. Raeburn could see for himself that Jimmy was the hub about which the life of the house turned. Mr. Raeburn saw this, and inwardly remarked to himself that it never had been thus at his own house.

With a great cheer Tom Willow had just announced that the roast venison was done to a turn, when a voice called rather faintly, "Father! Father! Are you there?"

Mr. Samuel Raeburn turned pale. He looked at the black window pane, and without consulting his watch he knew instantly how much time had flowed behind him since he had left the gun shop to gather up Jimmy and march the truant home by the ear!

But as he sat there, rather pale and cold, realizing what he had done—or rather, what he had *not* done—young Barry Litton hastily sprang out through the doorway. He found the girl standing at the edge of his rented ground, leaning a hand upon one of his trespass signs.

"We're waiting for nothing but you," he said. "Come along in."

"There is supper waiting at home," said the girl. "I'll go back."

"You'll come in," said Blue Barry. "Please!"

"Good food ought not to be wasted," said she.

"Exactly," insisted Litton. "And we have tons more than we can use. You see, Jimmy did the ordering, and you'll have to help us do the eating!"

His hand took her arm. His will fell upon her with a gentle compulsion. In a moment she was inside the door.

"Lou is here to join us!" exclaimed Blue Barry in a cheerful voice. "How's that for a good fellow?"

And there she was in the kitchen, with Jimmy dancing around her, and her father looking at her with eyes wide with a mixture of guilt and pleasure and surprise.

Tom Willow, mopping his brow with a bandanna, was thundering, "Hey, come and get it—come and get it—Jimmy, gimme some of that hot water—sit down here. You're here, sir. On his right, Miss Raeburn. You're here, Mr. Raeburn. I'll be along soon as I get some sand soap and hot water after my hands. That doggone venison grease sure sinks in!"

Lou was in her place before she knew, altogether, how she got there; and the stranger was talking cheerfully with her father. Jimmy was pinching her, and whispering in her ear, "Look at him, Lou. Ain't he wonderful?"

She hardly heard the words. She was tingling from head to foot. She wanted to be angry, but she felt that she could not find anger in her soul. She wanted to escape, and yet she dreaded nothing more than leaving. She had a feeling that she was captive here, and yet there was a sweetness in it such as freedom could never have.

She looked straight before her as Blue Barry said, "Your coming makes it a real party, Lou.—It's a regular house-warming!"

She had to frown a little at that, for she felt that a smile, just then, might be dangerous; she could not tell why.

8. THREE BIRDS WITH ONE JOLT

TWO THINGS WERE OF MOMENT—THE COOKING OF TOM Willow and the assiduity of Jimmy as a waiter.

Said Mr. Samuel Raeburn, "You've done something to Jimmy, Litton. There's a boy that can't open more than one eye at a time, when he's home. If he's got to chop some kindling, he develops the blind staggers. If he has to carry in some wood, he has rheumatism. If it's milking the cow, his hands are laid up for weeks afterwards."

"Why," said Tom Willow, "this is the way of it: a kid at home don't feel that he gets any glory out of bein' good. What's the use? The rest of his family is swore in to love him, like witnesses is swore in at a trial. Why be useful to folks like that? There ain't any use.—Just hand me a mite of a slice of that fried sweet potato, Jimmy, will you?—But in a strange house a boy takes and wakes up. And in a strange house a boy ain't weighted down by no family love."

It was in the middle of the party that Mr. Raeburn asked why the electric light was not on in the front room, and Jimmy said, "He's got a contraption that runs outside from the light—"

At that very moment a loud yell burst on them from the direction of the corral, and at the same time the light went dim in the kitchen. Two or three pistol shots followed, in rapid succession, from beyond the house, and then several piercing cries of pain.

Barry Litton was out the door in an instant, with a gleam of steel in his hand. Jimmy ran in pursuit, but when he gained the scene, the main action had ended.

Up the road, and across the open country on all sides, certain shadowy forms of horsemen were disappearing; and on the ground near the corral, dazed, and slowly writhing, three men were found. One of these last was the huge form of Jerry Deacon; one was young Harry Morgan; and one was big Rush Morgan himself!

Swiftly, while they were yet dazed, Barry Litton tied the three hand to hand, and relieved them of their guns. They could barely stagger down the street, escorted by Litton and Raeburn and Jimmy, until all were standing in the little front room of the sheriff's house, with the sheriff himself puffing at his long-stemmed pipe and looking them over.

"Thieves, sheriff," said Litton, "caught red-handed trying to steal the Dead Man Steer."

"You lie!" shouted Rush Morgan, who had recovered to some extent. "And what's more, you lie in your heart. It's only a dirty hound that puts a live wire around a corral fence and pretty near kills three honest men—"

"Hold on," said the sheriff, who rarely saw a point, but now began to make one out. "Hold on! What was three honest men doin' in the dark of the moon, on ground that had a sign out agin trespassers? And what was they doing around a corral that had the Dead Man Steer inside of it?"

Rush Morgan cried out, "Are you takin' the side of this young crook?"

"Crook?" exclaimed the sheriff. "You be careful what kind of talk you sling around here, Morgan."

"A good-for-nothin', worthless—" began Rush Morgan.

Big Sam Raeburn closed upon Morgan. "You never saw the day, Morgan," said he, "when you were worth the shady side of his little finger."

"You, too, Raeburn, eh?" cried the cattleman, enraged past endurance. "You're takin' up with strangers and interlopers, are you?—I'll tell you what I'll do. I'll break you, for this—and I'll break you flat!"

"Will you?" answered the other. "Then you start in breaking early, and get at it hard. You've run this town long enough, you Morgans, and it's time that some real men took a hand!"

"Pinch 'em! Run 'em in!" exclaimed a sharper voice.

This was Jimmy, dancing everywhere in the foreground, and listening to every exciting word that was spoken.

"Pinch 'em," said the sheriff, "is what I gotta do. But I don't need no kids around to tell me my duty."

"Sheriff," said Rush Morgan, "you mean to say that you're gonna take me to your dirty jail—?"

"Dirty jail?" said the sheriff, angrily. "Dirty jail, is it? It's the cleanest and the most upstandin' jail that you ever was in in your life, and you know it! It's one of the best jails that ever was run free in the West. Dirty jail, eh? I tell you, it's too damned good for you and the likes of you.—March along, the three of you! To jail you go, and in jail you stay till the law lets you out!"

Rush Morgan was instantly sobered. He cried, "A man of my age—You wouldn't wanta—I can't go to jail, Dick. My Lord, it'd ruin me—!"

"Then you're ruined," said the sheriff, bluntly. "If cattle lifting don't ruin you, then jail shall!"

At the corral beside the shanty, Lou Raeburn stood with Willow, staring at the looming bulk of the Dead Man Steer.

"You know, Tom," said the girl, "your chief has some of the strongest men in the county against him, and he hasn't yet spent a whole day in Holy Creek."

"Know it?" said Willow. "Sure I know it. I know it so good that I expect a slug of lead through me almost any minute, and a flock of cowpunchers comin' at me through the darkness like a pile of wild Injuns."

"What does *he* gain from it?" asked the girl.

"Him? Litton?"

"Yes."

"He gets the thing he wants the most."

"What's that?"

"Trouble!" said Tom Willow with a great deal of fervor in his voice. "I've seen him goin' around the world, huntin' for trouble; and that's a thing that anybody could find, almost with his eyes shut, d'ye see?"

"That's what I've always thought," said she.

"And it's true!" said Tom Willow. "They say that them that wants trouble are always sure to get as much as they can hold. But that don't work for Barry Litton. There ain't enough trouble in the world, for him. I don't know what he'd heard about this place, but—here we are."

"That's hard on you—following a fellow like that?" she suggested.

"You bet it's hard!"

"It's a free country," said the girl. "Why do you stay on with him, if it's so bad?"

He scratched his head noisily and stared at her for a moment. "Why," said he, "I never even thought about that. I suppose I *could* walk out on him."

"Of course you could."

He shook his head, soberly. "No, I couldn't do it," he declared. "It wouldn't seem nacheral to be without him and by myself."

"No?" she queried, smiling at him.

"It's like this," explained Tom Willow. "When you been hitched onto the tail end of a comet for a while, no other kind of travelling don't seem to satisfy you. If I left him, I'd always seem to be standing still."

She laughed; the cortège was returning from the jail. Jimmy came running up to his sister.

"Ever see anything like him?" he cried. "He went and run electricity into the barbed wire that Tom strung around the corral, and now he's got three of the Morgan outfit, and it didn't cost him a penny apiece! Why, he could catch stars out of the sky, if he sets his mind to it! —My Lord, ain't the whole town gonna bust out laughin' when it hears about how the Morgans been rounded up?"

The girl, however, found no more laughter in her. "He'll come to rest before long," she declared.

"Where?" asked her brother.

"In the graveyard at Boot Hill," said she. "Jimmy, we have to go home." And she slipped away into the darkness even before Litton had come up.

9. A LONG TRAIL

BARRY LITTON HAD BEEN DELAYED AT THE JAIL BY
the sheriff, who persuaded him to accept a deputy's
badge.

"Why," said the sheriff, "you're doin' a deputy's job
right now. And you're doin' it doggone good. When the
Morgans get through with this mess they're gonna remember barbed wire. They're gonna be laughed at by the
whole range, and there ain't nothing like laughter to boil
down the size of a fathead. Wait till I swear you in. A
coupla deputies like you, and I'll have this chunk of the
range comin' to church of a Sunday!"

There on the spot he swore in Barry Litton and
pinned a badge inside the lapel of his coat. It was a moment which the sheriff would have reason to remember,
and so would the entire county, and other counties beyond.

On the steps of the jail they parted.

"I'm gonna sleep here at the jail," said the sheriff.
"If the Morgan boys try to get their pals out of jail—if
they come with their whole gang—I'll turn loose on 'em
with riot guns. I'll cool 'em off, I tell you. I know that I
got public opinion behind me now, Litton. You waked
it up; it's been havin' a sleep for a long, long time. A
sheriff without public opinion behind him, he's like a dog
that's gone and lost all his teeth!"

So Barry Litton went back to his house with a long,
light stride, walking, as always, in the very middle of the
street, so that the slightest turning of his head would
show him the houses on either side, for a considerable
distance behind him. His heart was light, and therefore
his step was quick and eager, and he was humming softly
to himself, when he came back to the house which he
had taken from Si Turner.

Yonder in the corral was the focal point upon which

51

many a wave of danger and trouble was sure to break before long—the Dead Man Steer. But his glance failed to find it.

He turned with a frown. The steer was not there! What could Tom Willow have done with it?

"Tom!" he called.

The sound of his voice spread out around him, and died away. It brought back to him no answer.

A gun slid into his hands, instinctively. "Tom—oh, Tom Willow!" he called again.

From a corner of the house, a pair of rifles now spoke in reply—rifles that chattered busily and filled the air around him with a song of lead. He dropped to his face and lay still.

"We got him," said a voice, near the house.

"I'll go and see."

"Never mind seeing. He's dead. I fair caught him in the middle with a coupla slugs. He was right up agin the stars, for me!—That's the end of one bright gent. Let's grab the hosses and slide along because the shootin' may raise a crowd."

Their voices died out.

Litton, instantly on his feet, raced after them; but as he turned the corner of the house, he saw a pair of horsemen already mounted and swaying off at full gallop into the night.

He turned back. A revolver would not reach them at that distance—besides, there was Tom Willow. What had become of Tom?

Back to the corral he hurried, and as he neared the gate, he tripped on something soft. It was Tom Willow, lying on his face. Barry turned the limp bulk on its back.

"If he's dead, *I'm* the murderer!" said Blue Barry, through his teeth.

He placed an ear against Willow's breast, but almost at once he heard the steady, strong beating of the heart. He picked the massive burden up in his lean, powerful arms, and carried it back inside the house. Blood streaked down on either side of Tom's head, but his face was that of a man asleep, and having a bad dream. His lips curled, as though he was trying to get his teeth into something.

In ten minutes, Tom Willow was on his feet, with a bandage about his head and vengeance in his eye.

"They come up and socked me from behind," he said, bitterly. "They didn't give me a man's chance.—We gave *them* a chance. Yeah, we could of poked plenty of lead into the three that we found down, and nobody could of touched us for it. But we wouldn't be that snaky. We played straight, and all that we got was a slam over the head. I'm gonna do something about that, sir—if I gotta die the next minute."

"Go to bed, then, Tom," said his master. "We can't trail 'em in the dark, but we'll try our hands in the morning."

Unwillingly, Tom Willow turned in, but only after he had gone to the door and glowered at the thick of the dark.

In the first gray of the dawn he was in the kitchen, cooking breakfast; and before sunup the two men were on the trail, Willow on his mule, and the gray mare carrying big Barry Litton.

The trail they were to follow was that which the steer had left when it had been driven from the corral. Knowing about the electrified barbed wire, of course, it had been a simple matter to cut the cord that supplied the current. The trail led straight across the country for two miles. Then the tracks went down to a water hole, where they became lost among the spoor of ten thousand other cattle that had come there to drink.

The two men looked at this problem with a groan. Presently they backtracked, and found the sign of the two riders who had driven the steer. That made the offense the greater—the fact that it had been deemed that no more than two riders were needed for the deed. The horse of one of the riders was shod in the near forefoot with a shoe that was closed with a bar. That seemed an easy sign to follow, but when they returned to the water hole, the print disappeared among the myriad stampings and slitherings of other horse sign and cow sign.

The sun grew hot above the pair as they wandered about the trail, trying to pick up that mark of the barred shoe again, and failing.

Not until they cast out beyond the hill did they find the trail of the steer, and then the sign of another horse that had joined it. A quarter of a mile further on, the mark of the barred shoe rejoined the other two trails.

From this point, for a matter of several miles, they made good time over the trail; and then they descended into the bottom of a dry draw, covered with large stones. Here the trail went out completely.

They took to the banks, and hunted up and down, but this was difficult because of the number of tributary gulches with high, perpendicular banks, impossible for a horse to climb.

For two full hours they struggled over the problem, and the sun climbed to the center of the sky, growing more and more bright and hot. No breath of air was stirring. The walls of the narrow draws collected the heat and held it like liquid in a cup.

Only bulldog patience brought them to the place where the sign of the steer and the two riders cut in again from a side gulch and travelled across the level ground above. Barry and Tom passed through the burning grasslands, mile after mile, until they reached a fine grove of trees. Here a bit of a creek broke from a spring in the midst of the shade, and trickled away.

They rested, in grim silence. For it was plain that they could not hope to run down the thieves of the Dead Man Steer, considering the long number of hours that they had now lost. Besides, a long-legged steer is able to make some pretty long marches, and the thieves could be counted on to push the animal every step of the way.

Blue Barry Litton made the fire; Tom Willow performed as cook.

When they started again, a mist came in the northwest, turned red, darkened, and then there swept upon them a mighty sandstorm. They found a patch of rocks, made the mule and the horse lie down, and stretched out in the lee of the beasts, with handkerchiefs over their noses and mouths.

They waited until the stifling dust no longer whirled about them in such quantities. When they got up again, the wind was still strong and the dust was still flying, though not in such quantities as to make breathing and seeing impossible. Dust the color of rust had blown in from the desert, and for the time being the sun-dried grass was almost buried from sight, except that tufts of it rose now and again.

"There goes the trail," said Tom Willow, nodding. "And I ain't sorry. Trouble was gonna lie at the end of it, and as for that damn steer, I hope we never have to see the brute again!"

"We'll strike ahead and try our luck," said Litton, so they cast blindly ahead.

They struck on through the drifting dust, passing into a rift among some hills. This opened presently into a small, shallow depression, in the center of which grew half a dozen bedraggled trees, beside a heap of ruins.

"That's the end of to-day's march," said Barry Litton.

"It's the end of the whole search," said Tom Willow. "We ain't gonna find the sign again—not with this here red powder scattered all over the face of things."

Litton glanced at him impatiently, but made no answer; yet his glance told on Tom Willow. The sailor sighed, and looked with troubled eyes toward the sky and back to the ground. He knew what that tightening of the lips and glinting of the eyes meant.

The trees now seemed to thin out and grow smaller and more wretched. They drew closer to the ruins, which proved to be no more than a few decaying walls of 'dobe brick. But from the thickness of the walls it was plain that the building had once been of a considerable size. Weather had done to it what it will always accomplish on neglected 'dobe.

They unsaddled gloomily. The dust was still flying, and though there was still another hour before sunset, the entire sky began to take on a dingy hue of red, with greenish tinges in it, here and there. The wind continued to moan about them.

The horses had been tethered, when a voice spoke faintly out of the ground on which they stood. Faint as it was, they made out the words.

"Stand still there," it said. "Stand over, you doggone long-eared son of trouble!"

They stared at each other. Then, signing to Tom Willow to keep silent, Litton began scouting rapidly among the ruins.

Almost at once he found what he was looking for. A tunnel perhaps two yards wide and about the same in height, sloped sharply down into darkness below the surface of the ground. Following this, Barry was soon lost in a deep gloom. He felt his way, one hand resting against the wall, and so he came to a turning that gave him a dull glimmering of light.

Another turn, and he stood on the verge of a large, low-ceiled chamber, what had undoubtedly once been a cellar room. In the center of it was the dark mouth of a well, and at one side, contentedly munching at a pile of hay, there stood the Dead Man Steer. Its eyes were half closed, its long tail was swinging pendulously from side to side.

The design branded on its flank was clearly visible by the light of the lantern that hung on the wall, and beneath the lantern, his head bowed disconsolately on one hand, was an unshaven cowpuncher. He was a lean fellow of middle age, whose face seemed to have been dried up, like the skin of an apple left to wither in the sun.

Litton levelled his revolver, hip-high. "Well, partner?" said he.

The other started. But immediately he lifted his head very slowly, gradually turning it until he saw, first Barry and then the levelled gun.

"Yeah, I thought it'd be this way," he remarked, with a yawn.

"I said right from the start that it was no one-man job!"

"Stand up," commanded Litton.

"No sooner said than done," answered the cowboy, rising. With dull, disinterested eyes, he looked toward Litton.

"Unbuckle that gun belt and let it drop," commanded Litton. "Now hoist your hands, and turn your back to me."

"Got nothin' more on me," declared the other. Nevertheless he obediently raised his hands and turned his back.

Litton dexterously fanned him, and found that he spoke the truth.

"You can drop your hands, partner," said Litton, stepping back and lifting the fallen gun belt on the tip of his toe.

The cowpuncher faced him again.

56

"What's your name?" asked Litton.

"Mike Smith," said the weary-faced puncher.

"Who's the partner that helped you grab the Dead Man Steer away from me?"

"Him? I dunno nothin' about that. The steer was turned over to me on the range."

Litton smiled. "Where?"

"Coupla miles back— More than that. Maybe an hour's march."

Litton shook his head. "The same horses drove it the whole distance," he declared.

"I dunno nothin' about it," said Mike Smith.

"You will remember, though," said Litton. He raised his voice to a shout. "Tom! Oh, Tom! Come down here."

A faint cry answered him. He stepped over to the Dead Man Steer and rubbed his hand over its well-conditioned neck.

"I'll remember what?" asked the cowpuncher, frowning.

"Everything that I want to know," said Litton.

"A gent can't remember what he never knew," said the puncher, rather dubiously.

Tom Willow's voice boomed heavily down the passage. Litton answered, and presently the ex-sailor was with them. He grunted at the sight of the third man.

"This," said Litton, "is one of the two that batted you over the head, Tom. But he has already forgotten about that."

"Has he?" muttered Willow. "*I* ain't forgot it, though."

"Batted who over the head?" asked the puncher, blinking his eyes.

"He doesn't know a thing," said Litton. "But I'm going to stir his memory a little and see what may come of it. Tie his hands."

This was done, roughly and securely.

"Now," said Litton, "I'll go up on deck and get what I need to rouse him. We'll keep him down here; the yells won't sound very far that way!" He disappeared.

"What yells?" asked the puncher, in a startled voice.

"I dunno," grunted Willow.

"He said the yells wouldn't sound so far," said the other.

"Did he?" muttered Tom Willow.

"Yeah, he said that—and you heard him. What's he aim to do with me?"

"I dunno," said Tom Willow, "and I dunno that I care. He's a hard man, is Mr. Litton."

"He's hard, is he?"

"Even the Chink pirates that hang a gent up by his toes and burn out his eyes, one by one, and cut off his fingers, a joint at a time—even them Chinks used to think that Mr. Litton was a hard man; and a doggone hard man he sure is!"

"Is he?" gasped the prisoner. Fear seemed to make him younger, his eyes opened so far.

"Yeah, you can take what I say," said Tom Willow. "Hard is the word. But I don't give a rap what he does to you. You're the sneak that come up behind and slammed me, back there by the corral."

"Hold on! That wasn't me," said Mike Smith.

"Oh, you know that much, do you? You know it wasn't you? Who was it, then?"

"I dunno," said Mike Smith, sullenly.

"No?"

"I dunno nothin' about it."

"That's all right, too," said Tom Willow. "Mr. Litton understands how to make gents remember things. I recollect a pair of Solomon Islanders—and a mean, hard pair they were, too. They didn't know nothin', neither. But before he got through with 'em, they begun to remember; and along towards the end, they was talkin' faster than you could put their remarks down in shorthand."

"What did he do to them?" asked the puncher, agape with horror and with interest.

"I dunno," said Tom Willow. "Them are trade secrets of his; and what I've seen, I'm pretty glad to forget. But those islanders won't forget. What's left of the pair of 'em, that is, won't forget!"

"Lord A'mighty!" breathed the puncher.

"There was one," said Tom Willow in a reminiscent tone of voice, "that had only about half a face left to him. Still, I dunno but I pitied more the one that had had his tongue tore out of his throat."

The puncher swallowed visibly, and with difficulty.

At that moment, big Barry Litton came back, carrying

58

a quantity of wood in one arm and a rope and knife in the other. His wink to Tom Willow was hidden from the prisoner's view.

"We could stake him out here, right across the mouth of the well, Tom," suggested Litton, thoughtfully.

"Yeah, that would do.—You could drop the body in the well afterward, with a stone tied to it."

"That's a fair idea, but I hate to spoil a good well with a hound like him," declared Litton. "Sharpen up this knife for me, because I'm going to work fast. Here, you—Mike Smith, or whatever your name is—you don't remember anything, eh? Well, start to—"

"Wait a minute!" said a faint and husky voice. "I'll talk, brother—I'll talk! I didn't know you was an Injun under the skin!"

10. A HAUL OF CHANEYS

LITTON'S FACE DARKENED. "I DON'T KNOW," HE SAID. "I gave you your chance before. I ought to stick to my word now, and make trouble for you. I'm set and ready for it, and it's what you deserve.—Now, what's your real name?"

"Bud Lorrain."

"Is that straight, this time?"

"I swear it's the real name."

"Not Mike Lorrain, maybe?" sneered Litton.

"No, sir. It's Bud Lorrain."

"Who was your partner?"

"Steve Chaney."

"All right," said Litton. "Now you start at the beginning, and tell me what I want to know."

"The Judge called me in," said Lorrain. "Me and Steve."

"What judge?"

"Judge Chaney—Lawrence Chaney."

"And who's the Judge?"

"Why, he's the head of the Chaneys. He's the top mongul."

"Go on, then."

"The Judge called the pair of us in," said the other, "and he told us that the Chaneys had all been outraged, and things like that. If we sat still after we'd been insulted by the shootin' down of the Chaney cattle and feed sign, pretty soon, he said, the Chaney name would be kicked around in the dust, just the way folks was kicking the name of the Morgans around."

"Yeah," groaned Tom Willow. "With the half of a weather eye cocked to windward, I could of told that a pile of trouble would come out of shootin' down those two signs. What harm had *they* done to you, chief?"

"Be quiet, Tom," commanded Litton. "Let this fellow talk, because I can see that he's full of words."

"The Judge," went on the informant, "told us that he was hiring Rann Duval to come over and clean things up and put the steer where it belonged to be. Said he was ashamed to have a doggone tenderfoot litterin' up the landscape of *both* the Morgans and the Chaneys. The work that he wanted Rann to do would be with the Morgans."

"Who's Rann Duval?" asked Litton.

"I know part of that," said Tom Willow.

"Go on, Tom, and tell me what *you* know."

"Why," said Tom Willow, "I heard of him from a bunkie of mine that I run into in Singapore. He was down in Porto Rico in the old wild and woolly days. He seen a gang of the blacks jump Rann Duval on a wharf, and he seen Duval cut his way through 'em. Then Duval turned around and drove that gang of blacks in front of him, some of them droppin' along the way, till he made 'em jump into the water. He sat down on the pier head and smoked a cigar and took pot shots at their heads, bobbin' in the water."

"He sounds like quite a man," said Litton.

"He's one that can't miss," answered the prisoner simply. "I've seen him."

"Tell me some more about him," commanded Litton.

"With my own eyes, I seen him drop a steer at a thousand yards."

"Did you put a tape measure over the ground?" asked Litton.

"I paced it off."

"That's a long way to walk."

"I'd walk all day to see anybody shoot like that again," said Lorrain, his face lighting a little with the memory. "Why, it's pretty near like bein' the Almighty himself, to be able to reach over half a mIle away and pick off the gent that you want—just like that!"

"It's a long shot," said Litton gravely. "But go on with what our friend, the Judge, had to say."

"He said," continued Lorrain, "that he wanted something done while the excitement was still in the air, and while the town was laughing at the Morgans. That was the very time, he said, for us to step out and make a name for ourselves. The higher we hoisted ourselves, the deeper down the Morgans would go. So he said that he didn't want to use a whole crowd, the way the Morgans had done. Instead of that, he wanted only one or two men to go over and grab the steer and bring it here to this hole in the ground . . .

"Then we'd lay low with it for a while, and pretty soon we'd show it away off at the end of our part of the range, and the laugh would be on the Morgans for good, and also on the smart young gent that had knifed into the fights in Holy Creek.

"Well, we went up to Si Turner's place, and there we seen this gent here"—he pointed to Tom Willow—"standing guard by the gate, at the corral. We slipped up behind him, and Steve Chaney gave him a rap over the head with a sandbag—"

"Listen to him!" sighed Willow, gently touching his bandaged head. "That's what I call a crowd of real gentlemen—they carry sandbags around with 'em."

"If it had been the butt of a gun, it would have brained you, Tom," said the chief.

"I was just gonna remark that," said the prisoner ingratiatingly. "Well, we got the steer and started off. As we got it behind the house, we seen somebody comin' up the road, and I thought we might as well take a crack at him, too, and make it a good job."—He winced. "That was doggone wrong of me!" he admitted.

"I don't want pretty pictures. I want the true ones," said Litton. "Go right ahead."

"So we kept behind the corner of the house, and when the gent came near, we took him to be you, because he was headed right for the house. He hollered out for 'Tom,' so we let him have it. We must of ripped him in two, so it couldn't of been you, of course. I dunno what poor sucker it was. Then we sloped off to our hosses and herded the steer.—But you know all about that."

"We know about that," said Litton. "After you got along the trail, what became of Steve Chaney? Where is he now?"

"He rode straight across the hill to the Chaney ranch. The Judge had promised he'd be there, and he'll come back with Steve to have a look at the steer and to plan what next to do."

"How far to the ranch?"

"Why, about an hour."

"And how long ago did Steve start?"

"Close to two hours, chief."

Litton started. "They'll be back here any moment! Tom, go up and get the horses and ride like the devil till you've got them out of sight behind some hummock. It's too dark now for their tracks to be seen. Jump, Tom, and then come back here.—But come like a snake, as close to the ground as you can wriggle!"

Tom Willow, with a wave of the hand, departed. Minutes passed slowly.

A heavy voice called at the mouth of the tunnel, "Hey, Bud!"

Litton had barely finished pinioning the arms of his prisoner when that occurred.

"Answer up!" said Barry to his prisoner.

"Ahoy!" shouted Lorrain, a world of relief passing into his voice.

Footfalls approached.

"Ask if he has the Judge with him," said Litton.

"Got the Judge, Steve?" called the prisoner.

"Yeah, he's here," said a voice close at hand.

Two men turned the corner, the next instant, and almost ran against Litton's pair of guns.

"Steady up!" said Barry. "You're walking too fast!"

There was a second in which anything might have happened. Then the Judge set the example.

"Might's well put your hands up, Steve," said he with instant decision, and he raised his own hands above his head.

The Judge was rather an undersized man. Sitting, he must have been a commanding presence, for above the waist he was more than average, in size and height, with a great globe of a head and a fine face to which dignity was added by a trim gray beard, and well-tended mustaches. His was the sort of a face that painters choose to represent middle-aged gravity and wisdom.—What made him short when he was standing up was the absurdly disproportionate length of his legs.

His nephew, Steve Chaney, was a handsome young fellow with a resolute face—and a nature that mated his expression, for his hands went upward by small jerks, an inch at a time.

"Young fellow," said Steve Chaney, "I don't know what your game is, but we haven't much money on us. You can collect plenty out of us, though. Keep my uncle here, and I'll drop over to the ranch and get whatever you and the Judge agree on."

"That's quite right," said Judge Chaney. "The fact is—"

"How much will you offer, spot cash?" asked Litton curiously.

"A thousand dollars," said the Judge. "Hold on!" he added, seeing Litton's smile. "Seeing that there are a pair of us. I'll make it two thousand."

"Two for each of you?" asked Litton.

"Well then—though that's robbery—four thousand."

"No, six, including two for Bud Lorrain, here."

The Judge's lips compressed slightly. "Very well," he said slowly. "Six thousand dollars, then. But you'll have to wait until to-morrow for a part of that; I'll give you my note."

"Your note would be better than gold to me," said Litton. "Just sit down there and write out your note for the whole amount, will you?" He added, to the nephew, "Back over there, brother. Stand beside Lorrain, so that I can keep an eye on you."

Young Chaney took his place beside Lorrain, muttering.

The Judge, in the meantime, had kneeled; and putting an empty envelope on the edge of the casing of the wall, he drew from a pocket a bit of indelible pencil and rapidly wrote a note. He merely said, as he began, "Your name is Barry Litton?"

"That's the name."

"Here's my note," said the Judge, rising. "It calls for six thousand dollars, to be paid to Barry Litton. Is that right?"

"Perfectly right," said Barry Litton. "Now turn your back and I'll tie your hands."

There was a snarl of rage from Steve Chaney, but the Judge said calmly, "I see.—Just a bit of added highway robbery, eh? But that's all in the game."

"You've played the game so long that you understand it, eh?" said Litton. "You fellows march, now. It's a long distance back to town."

"Back to town!" exclaimed the Judge.

"That's what I said."

Chaney's face became bright with perspiration. "You don't mean that, my lad," said he. "A man of some rank and position in the society of the range—a man who—a life of honest endeavor—a. . . . In fact, Mr. Litton, I see that you will have to be reasoned with."

"But the truth is, Mr. Chaney," said Litton, grimly, "I don't see how you can do it!"

"Money talks," said the Judge. "I'll make you a flat offer. I'll give you ten thousand dollars, young man—a fine little fortune on which you can start in life according to a more honest and useful standard!"

"Ten thousand is a lot of money," answered Litton. "But it won't do."

"I'll raise the scale," said the Judge. "I'll revise my ideas. As a matter of fact, I see that you're a fellow standing a bit higher in your measurement of things than I guessed. We'll make it exactly double. I'll pay you *twenty* thousand dollars, Mr. Litton. Take this infernal rope off my hands, and I'll write out the note. Any bank on the range will cash that note!"

Litton smiled down at him. "I make up my mind, and my mind stays made," said he. "One note is all I want from you. You'll see why later on."

"I don't know what you mean by that," said the Judge.

"But, Litton, a little openness of mind on your part—"

He was cut off short by Litton, who exclaimed harshly: "Do you remember Red Pete?"

"Ah," said the Judge, "that unfortunate young man!"

"He was my friend," said Litton. "Will that shut up your talk about money?"

The Judge moved his lips. No words came.

Litton added, "The Chaneys and the Morgans have had their way too long in Holy Creek. Now they're going to taste law for a while; and law has a cold taste between the teeth, Judge. Like steel.—March out of here!"

He herded the three out from underground, and into the dimness of the twilight above. Willow had already returned with the horses. He went down now, at Litton's order, and drove up the Dead Man Steer. Then they started for Holy Creek, with the Chaneys tied to the backs of their horses.

11. A COUPLE OF CROOKS

CATTLE TOWNS WAKEN EARLY, AND THERE WAS AL-ready a stir of life in the town of Holy Creek when a small boy rode a scampering mustang through the streets, in the rose of the morning.

He was shouting at the very top of his lungs, "Turn out! Turn out!—Barry Litton's at it again! Turn out! Barry Litton's putting on another show!—Hey! Barry Litton's coming again."

That small, sharp voice, far-reaching as the crowing of a rooster, cut into the sleep of many a man and many a woman and child, and jerked them all from their beds.

It was Jimmy Raeburn who had raised the town. Sleep had not come to him during the night after he had discovered that Blue Barry, Willow, and the Dead Man Steer had all disappeared. The first gray of the morning had roused him before the chickens were off their roosts,

65

and he had cantered out of town like a restless young Indian, to scan the landscape. That was how he happened to see the cavalcade coming in the distance. He drew near enough to recognize the faces—then he whirled and raced for the town, to spread the tidings.

Man, woman and child thronged out into the streets. Straight to the sheriff's house had gone little Jimmy Raeburn, and his crowing voice tumbled the sheriff out of bed, reaching for his boots with one hand and his hat with the other. He was out instantly.

"Barry Litton's got 'em again—a few Chaneys, this time, and the Judge at the top of the list. Got 'em redhanded—and the Dead Man Steer is back in town!" yelled Jimmy Raeburn.

The sheriff had barely time to cinch a saddle on the back of his best horse and get to the jail, when he saw a multitude coming down the street. For Holy Creek had found a hero. The handling of Jerry Deacon, the guarding of the Dead Man Steer, the dropping of the Chaney and the Morgan signs, the capture of the three Morgan clansmen—all had followed rapidly, during the course of a mere half day.

Now Barry Litton was riding through the streets of the town, bearing with him three of the Chaney outfit. And, as had happened with the Morgans, one of the new prisoners was the very crown and head of the entire tribe. The chief of the Chaneys appeared with his feet lashed under the belly of his favorite saddle horse, and his hands tied behind his back.

Grimly, Judge Chaney kept his head high and his glance straight before him; but there was agony in his face. His title of judge had been conferred upon him not because he had ever been a judge, but because the public universally felt that he needed some title of respect. Now the great man had come to this!

There was no longer any fear in Holy Creek. Public opinion burst into laughter and cheering; here and there a single voice roared out above the rest: "We'll have no more gang rule! We'll have the law!"

"The law and Barry Litton!"

"Murder needs the rope!—They're murderers, the lot of 'em!"

The sheriff heard, and he ground his teeth. The ease

with which this blue-eyed daredevil had stolen the thunder of the Chaney-Morgan crowds and passed the ringleaders into the hands of the law was bound to reflect upon the sheriff himself shortly. What had the duly elected officer of the law been doing all this time?

Down came the swarm to the steps of the jail, and there the sheriff met them. The crowd was instantly hushed as Barry Litton stood up like a Tartar in his saddle. A small bit of paper fluttered in his hand. It marked his gestures as he spoke.

He said, very briefly, "Friends, the Dead Man Steer was stolen, and we followed the trail till it led us to this pair of Chaney aces. And to give you a proof—if you need a proof beyond the fact that he and his nephew are here, caught red-handed, along with the Dead Man Steer—I have still more to show.

"First, this man Judge Chaney is a cattle thief; and second, he plotted and planned a cowardly attack on Tom Willow, and then tried to murder me, just as he's tried to murder others before me. I have here in my hand a note for six thousand dollars, signed by his hand, which he tried to use to bribe me!"

That was more than enough. The sheriff, who understood public signs when he saw them written in the sky, so to speak, hastily caught hold of the two Chaneys and hustled them up the steps and through the front door of the jail.

Even so, with all his haste, he was barely in time, for as he slammed the door and threw home the heavy bolt, a score of hands struck against it as the first wave of the crowd reached for the prisoners.

Long and loud the voice of the maddened people yelled, "Lynch—lynch 'em! Lynch the Chaneys and the Morgans! We'll have law, and not murder!"

During that hubbub, young Barry Litton slipped away to Si Turner's house with Tom Willow. And when the crowd turned to look for its heroes, it found them gone. But in a fury of enthusiasm, the townsmen burst into prolonged cheering and marched for an hour up and down the street, as though following a flag.

Peace had fallen from the skies upon Holy Creek. It really did not pay to conduct a feud when the chiefs on both sides were apt to find themselves in jail, and would then have to pay ten thousand dollar bails before they could have their freedom!

In every case, the charges were serious. Cattle lifting was the least of them. Burglary, assault with intent to kill, bribery, blackmail, such items as these entered the list. It began to appear that the Morgans and the Chaneys were not the Lords of Creation after all; they seemed to be not even the Lords of Holy Creek!

In a word, Holy Creek began to take itself seriously, and it was glad that it had a man like Blue Barry Litton as a citizen.

To no one did the change mean as much as to Jimmy Raeburn. If his father said sharply to him, at night, "Why wasn't that wood chopped?" he had only to answer, "Barry Litton wanted me over at his place to—"

Well, it hardly mattered what he was wanted for. The name of Barry Litton had a magic force in the Raeburn household, and Jimmy was Barry's chosen friend. It made his father smile and nod; it made his sister smile and blush a little. Moreover, grown men took Jimmy seriously for the first time, hailed him on the street, and inquired from him the latest news concerning Barry Litton and the Dead Man Steer.

For the steer, like a mysterious emblem, now represented the reign of law and order. If it should be lost to one of the warring clans again, then it was felt that the reign of disaster would recommence.

Much as Jimmy Raeburn worshiped his new friend, there were some things about him that troubled the boy. For instance, Barry Litton never talked either about his past or his future. He never suggested that he might one day enter upon a career as a cattleman. He had simply appeared in the town of Holy Creek as a transient. He threatened to put an end to the great cattle war, but he was merely the last and finest flower of that excitement.

So Jimmy Raeburn was puzzled, and having many of the instincts of a red Indian, he decided to watch his friend when his friend was unaware of the eye that followed him. For Jimmy was young enough not to be worried by certain finer and higher moral and ethical scruples.

It was entirely owing to this that Jimmy happened to observe Barry from covert, when the boy's hero left the old Si Turner place at the end of one golden day and stepped out across the fields. The boy followed, and seeing Blue Barry enter Boot Hill Cemetery, he followed, worming his way from mound to mound and from shrub to shrub, until he saw that Barry Litton was sitting beside a grave that was not many months old.

The boy knew that grave well. He knew every inch of Boot Hill, as a matter of fact. He had spent countless hours there on sunny days, reading the names on the little wooden crosses, some of them merely written with pencil. He had felt it a pleasant but a rather grisly duty, now and then, to take an indelible pencil with him, and to freshen certain of the names that were growing illegible.

But Barry Litton was not doing anything about the grave; he was merely sitting beside it, with his lean, powerful arms wrapped around his knees. Sometimes he glanced at the wooden cross at the head of the grave, on which was written:

Here Lies
PETER CHALMERS
Known as Red Pete
Shot by Accident

The boy knew the phrasing of that legend word for word. He wondered what could cause the great Barry Litton to spend so much time beside that grave, buried in such deep thought. He was still wondering, when he saw another man stepping lightly among the graves and cautiously approaching his friend.

This last was a little man with a very brown face. He was thin, and he wore the get-up of a gambler—one of those wide black hats and a longish coat. His boots were polished so that the westering sun flashed on them with every step that he made. He wore a glove on his left hand, and the same hand clasped the glove for the right, a fact which seemed very strange to the boy.

When he was close to Barry Litton, this silent-stepping stranger made a long pause; and for some reason Litton, whose senses were usually so acute, failed to notice him. That seemed to Jimmy Raeburn the strangest thing of all.

It was only after a long moment that Litton turned his head with a jerk, saw the boots, and then, with a start, the face of the little man. "Good God!" gasped Barry Litton. "Stacey!"

The little man smiled, and raised a thin finger to his thin lips. "Not here, Barry!" said he. "Not that name here!"

"There's no one to hear it," said Barry Litton.

"There are the dead, Barry," said the other. "And some of 'em would be apt to turn over in their graves—or even jump out of 'em—if they heard it."

"What's the name nowadays?" asked Barry Litton, rising to his feet.

"Rann Duval," replied the small man.

The name went like a bullet through the mind of the listening Jimmy. Rann Duval had not been long on the range, but he was one of those men who made history with every lifting of his hand. He could hardly part his lips, it appeared, without saying things that other people would remember.

"Rann Duval, eh?" said Barry Litton. "You've made that name stick in the mind of these people, Stacey."

"Hush!" said the other, with his thin, cold smile. "Not that name, please—that goes only for another part of the world."

"The South Seas will remember it for a while," suggested Litton.

"And I shall remember the South Seas," said the small man, gravely.

"Got too hot out there for you?" asked Litton.

"Very hot," said Rann Duval.

Duval was saying, "It got a little warm for you and Chalmers out there, too, before the end."

"A little warm," agreed Barry Litton.

"That why you're back here?"

"No," said Litton. "Chalmers came from this part of the world. So did I. That's what made us partners, in the old days."

"Not so old, at that," said the other.

"Old for Chalmers," sighed Barry Litton.

"Nothing could ever be old for that red-head," answered Rann Duval.

"He's dead," said Litton, briefly.

The little man whistled. "Too bad!" he said. "You and Red Pete were always on the opposite side of the

70

fence from me, but I liked him. I liked him—" He paused.

"You liked him the better of the two, eh?" smiled Litton.

"I didn't want to be rude," said the little man. He had a soft, gentle voice that stole upon the ear almost like a whisper.

It made people lean a little to hear what he had to say.

Rann Duval was unlike any human being that little Jimmy Raeburn had ever seen or ever dreamed of. A feeling of awe came over the boy; it was like sitting alone in a cold dark house, when winter winds are whistling outside, and creaking ghostly footfalls go stealing through the halls.

"That's all right," said Litton. "I know how you stand about me, Stacey—Duval, I mean to say. But I never could make out just why you hated me so much."

"Couldn't you?" murmured the other.

"No," said Litton.

"Shall I tell you?"

"Yes, let me know about it."

"It's because," said Rann Duval, "you're one of the crooks who doesn't know he's a crook."

"Oh, I know I'm a crook, all right," said Litton.

"You don't," said Rann Duval. "You're one of the sort that keeps telling yourself that one day you'll go straight—you'll never do that, but you keep on telling yourself you will. And it makes you feel superior to dyed-in-the-wool thugs like myself, for instance."

"I feel that you're poison, and that I'm only partly poison," answered Litton. "Put it that way."

"That's the way you'd put it," said Duval. "And so I've dropped out here to-day to have a little chat with you."

"What about?"

"About the size of this part of the world. It seems big and roomy, but I've decided that it's too small to hold the pair of us!"

12. MAN OR DEVIL?

IT SEEMED TO JIMMY RAEBURN THE MOST RIDICULOUS thing in the world that a little fellow like Rann Duval should dare to stand up to the great Blue Barry and tell him that any part of the world was too small to hold both of them. A fluttering lightness that might have preceded laughter came into the throat of the boy.

Barry Litton, however, was not laughing. He looked with a great deal of consideration upon the smaller man, saying, "If this range is crowded, then I have to move. Is that it?"

"I hate to talk like a sheriff and ask you to move on," said Rann Duval.

"Yes, I know how you hate it," murmured Litton. He stooped, picked up a number of pebbles, and began to flick them to a distance, one by one, with a snap of his thumb. Litton looked at ease, mildly thoughtful; there was only a slight twitch at the corner of his lips that enabled the boy to guess what pressure was on his soul.

Amazement began to freeze up the heart of the youngster. Barry Litton, it appeared, was not going to stretch forth his hand and cause the smaller man to disappear, after all.

"But," went on Rann Duval, "moving seems to be the best idea. I wasn't sure, until I trailed you here to Boot Hill."

"Weren't you?" asked Litton.

"No, but now I am."

"That's not very clear," said Barry Litton.

"Isn't it?" said the other. "Look at this, then: I come here almost half glad to see you—in spite of the fact that you and Chalmers won a game from me in the old days. You had beginner's luck, and I was willing to overlook it, perhaps. It seemed pleasant to meet somebody who could chatter about blackbirds, so to speak."

72

He laughed a little as he spoke. His laughter was as soft as his speech, but even after it had ceased, chilly tricklings continued to run through Jimmy Raeburn's spinal marrow.

Rann Duval went on. "Then I come out and see this—see you sitting on the ground by the grave of Red Pete. Well—" He paused with a very slight, very elegant gesture that included the lifting of one shoulder.

"Makes you a little sick, eh?" said Litton. "The hypocrisy of it?"

"You had to do it," said Rann Duval. "You're that sort. Even when there wasn't an audience, you had to go through with the silly, crooked play, in order to convince *yourself* that you are a white man! You wanted to have a chance to write down this moment in your secret heart, as one of the good moments, one of the big ones. It would be a comfort to you to the end, I'm sure."

"Would it?" murmured Litton.

"Yes," said Rann Duval. "This is the point about you: you're one of those fellows who are surprised when they die and find themselves in hell."

"By gad!" murmured Litton. "You hate me, Stacey, don't you?"

"I don't like to use that word—hate," said Duval. "It's an awfully strong word to use to an old blackbirder like you, but I'm afraid that I'll have to use that—or something like it."

"Quite all right," said the other.

"Well?" said Stacey-Duval, sharply. He raised his brows and waited for the answer.

"You make me thoughtful," said Litton. "I thought I had at least a little courage, but I don't seem to have that, even."

"No. We can be honest, here," said Duval. "That's why I was glad to get a chance to speak to you alone. That damned freckle-faced brat is generally around to spoil the landscape."

A greater thrill than ever went through Jimmy Raeburn.

"Being alone," said Duval, "you don't have to fight. Of course I know that you wouldn't let yourself be publicly shamed. That's not the point.—Suppose you merely get a hurry call to another part of the globe. I've arranged all of that. Just say the word, and before to-morrow morning you'll get a telegram from New York, urging you to come. Then your face is saved."

"I go to the sheriff, and tell him that I can't keep on with the Dead Man Steer, eh?"

"Of course."

"I hand over my badge?"

"Or keep the thing. All I want is for you to step off the stage."

"How well are you paid for this, Stacey?" asked Litton.

"You shouldn't ask about that. It's my private business, but also it's my private pleasure."

"You're as frank as can be," remarked Litton, "and I'm grateful. You're a fool if you don't stick both the Chaneys and the Morgans for several thousand.—But then, you'll want to stay with one side, and be used to get the Dead Man Steer itself, after I'm off the stage."

"All details that don't concern you," said Duval, gently.

"No doubt.—Still, I'm interested. Interested in the idea of the great Stacey turning cowpuncher. How several tens of thousands of islanders would laugh if they could see you swinging a rope!" He chuckled.

The laughter seemed an honest, unforced sound; and it brought relief to the heart of Jimmy Raeburn.

Still—why didn't Litton strike the scoundrel to the ground? Was Duval really a devil? Had he mysterious powers?

"Well?" said Duval. "Well, Barry?"

"I can't help sticking on one point."

"Tell me. I may be able to help you slide off it."

"The Dead Man Steer."

"Are you joking, Barry?"

"I'm not joking. I'm interested in the Dead Man Steer. You'd laugh if I told you why."

"I'm not laughing just now," said the other.

"It's this way," remarked Litton. "I'm interested in keeping that steer away from the thugs; I've made a moral issue of it. You say I'm a rotten hypocrite. Perhaps I am. I have a queer feeling in my bones that if I can back up the law in this job, and beat the cruel devils who killed Pete Chalmers, I'd half save that soul of mine—which, as you were just saying, is overdue in hell."

"Your brain is a little twisted," said Duval. "Let me help to unravel the strings and put the thing in order. You leave the town, and you're covered up, and nobody is allowed to suspect that I've driven you away—nobody except my paymaster, whoever he may be. Is that clear to you?"

"Clear as the ringing of a bell," replied the other.

"Or," Duval added, "you don't go, and I prepare you for one of these little plots."

"That's clear, too," said Litton.

"Well?" Duval demanded.

"I hate to give up the Dead Man Steer," said Litton. "You're an older and a cleverer man than I am, Duval. You're a better shot, and a faster hand with a gun. You're everything that a first class murderer ought to be. Still—"

"My dear Barry," said the smaller man, "now you touch me!—Now you stir my heart!"

"But in spite of the fact that I'm as much afraid of you as I would be of a fiend in flames, the Dead Man Steer continues to hold me."

"Perhaps you'll give him another reason for his name. *That* may be on the books."

"Maybe. I've got to have a little time to think it over."

"Take ten minutes."

"I'll need an hour or two."

"It's too long."

"No," said Litton. "You're a better man than I am in a fight. But I was always good, and I've improved since that day when you saw me working for my life. I've improved, and you know it. You won't pull a gun on me as long as you think that persuasion may work. You'll give me a couple of hours.—Till nine o'clock, say?"

"All right," said the other, with a sudden gesture. "But why can't you tell me now? Why all this rot about the Dead Man Steer, and service to society, and all of that?"

"There is another thing; you irritate me, Duval."

"I'm glad to hear you say it!" said Duval. "It sounds more honest."

"I'm going home now," said Litton. "I'll take till nine o'clock to tell you whether I'll be wise and leave town, or whether I'll be a fool and stay on."

Duval glanced towards the sunset.

"Oh, all right," he said. "I'll drop around about nine o'clock and find out how you feel. If you have a lamp in the window at nine, I'll know that you've made up your mind to leave. If it's not in the window, the music begins to play. Is that satisfactory?"

"Perfectly," said Litton.

"Adios," murmured Duval, and turning on his heel, he walked jauntily down the path among the graves.

It seemed more than strange. It was true that Litton was not the fellow to shoot from behind, but how could the other be sure of it? So Jimmy watched the departing figure, and then fastened his glance on his friend. Then a frightful shock struck his brain. For as he watched, the great Barry Litton, with a gesture as light as a feather, brought into his hand a huge blue-barreled revolver and stood with it hip-high, covering the retreating form.

A red haze dimmed Jimmy's sight; all his belief in mankind crashed in the dust as he stared; and then, as when a bad dream ends happily, he saw the gun vanish from the hand of his friend.

He had hardly begun to breathe again, when he saw Duval's small form turn briskly about. His hat was raised with a distinct flourish, and he sang out, "Thank you, Barry!"

Then he turned and went on again, with that light, springy step, rising lightly on his toes as though there was some spirit in him greater than his body could contain.

As for Barry Litton, he did not walk on again. Instead, as his enemy disappeared, he sank down on the grave-mound of Peter Chalmers and remained with his head buried in his hands until the cold of the twilight drew about him. Then he stood up and went slowly home.

13. THE LIGHT IN THE WINDOW

JIMMY RAEBURN'S HEART HAD BEEN AS A FLAME DURING all of these days. It was now leaden within him, and as the big man moved away Jimmy lay like one who has been wounded. The boy had a desperate feeling that something must be done, and at once; but he could not tell what the proper thing might be. Then he thought of the gloom of the darkened little house to which his hero would be returning.

But Barry was a hero no longer. He had been reduced, at one stroke, to the stature of ordinary men. Jimmy was hollow with grief. It was like homesickness, only much worse.

As he struggled to his knees, he told himself that now he was a man—for was he not always hearing his elders speak of the pain that comes only with years? It seemed to him that they had come to him—the years and their pain—in one bitter rush. Barry Litton was not a flawless hero; he was a fellow who *could* feel fear for another man, another mortal man. Furthermore, the dastardly thought of shooting another in the back *could* enter his brain, and had.

Jimmy began to wonder if that little fellow, that terrible little man Duval, might not be right after all in his bitter judgment of Litton.

In the meantime, Litton must not be allowed to go home to a house that contained no face more cheerful than that of Tom Willow, for Tom was always apt to be a grouchy fellow, when he was busy cooking a meal.

Like a hawk on the wing, Jimmy cut around the striding form of Litton, almost lost in the darkness, and reached the shack of Si Turner ahead of Barry.

"Hello," said Tom Willow, as Jimmy entered. "I could tell dinner-time like a clock was strikin', by the time that you come in. And around about the time that there's wood to be chopped and chores to be done, why, that's the time that there ain't any Jimmy to be found. I can stand out there and bray for Jimmy like a mule, but I wouldn't raise no more than an echo—and a damned weak echo at that. But here you are, bright and shinin' like the face of a lead dollar with gilding on it. The kids these days are spoiled. They're a lazy lot of little brats, and that's why the world is goin' down hill. Here, take and slice these potatoes into that pan, and slice 'em thin, mind you!"

Anger was in Jimmy's heart, but his duty on this evening was to smooth over troubled waters. Carefully, he set to work on the potatoes.

"Hey, wash your hands, first—an' wash them potatoes, after. Where was you raised? In a barn?" shouted Tom Willow.

The boy's hands were dutifully washed, but Jimmy ground his teeth in silence. "I guess you were brought up pretty careful, Tom," he suggested after a time.

"I was brought up *right*," said Tom Willow. "If I turned out wrong, it ain't the fault of them that raised me, I can tell you, because they done a job on me and they done it right."

"I'll bet they did," said the boy. His amiable consent caused Tom Willow to jerk his head about and stare over his broad shoulder, glowering. What was this kid driving at?

But Jimmy met him with round and innocent eyes. Not the archangels of heaven—not even the archfiends of hell—can penetrate the guile of a twelve-year-old boy.

"I'll tell you how I was raised," said Tom Willow, "and a doggone good thing if your pa took you in hand the same way. I was raised in a house where there was a willow switch in every room, so's it'd be handy. 'Spare the rod and spoil the child,' the sayin' goes.—And they never spared the rod, lemme tell you. They wore 'em to rags, and me to blisters.—Hurry up with them potatoes!— I was a kid, Jim, that would jump a block, when my pa or my ma spoke to me. Ma was the handier of the two. When pa turned loose, he certainly cut down to the quick, but ma was kind of more steady and regular. She was a pile more thoughtful, too. I mean, she was always thinking of new things for me to do. I was raised, Jim,

78

so's I was a credit to the family. I kind of fell off, later on, but that was my own fault. Because when I got on my own, I thought this doggone world was kind of too small for a bird as fast on the wing as me, and I tried to fly all the way round it, a coupla times a day."

This oration had improved Tom Willow's spirits, so that when Barry Litton came in, his temper was very good, indeed.

He sang out, "Say, Barry, you never told me how you was raised. Let's hear that!"

Litton stood with his hand on the knob of the door, which he had just closed behind him. His face was pale. His glance had lowered. Yet there was a smile on his face as he answered, "Why do you want to know, Tom?"

"Well, just to help make you out," said the ex-sailor. "What gave you your start at home?"

"I'll tell you," said Barry Litton, "and here's an example for all parents to follow. I was raised on love. If I wanted anything, I got it. If I wanted to dodge anything, I lied out of it. And when my lies were found out, my parents said that it was just a child's fault, which I would outgrow. Yes, it was all love, around my house.—And you see the result? That's why I grew up so fine and straight. That's why I've got so many friends that a king would be proud to know. That's the reason, my boys, that I have money in the bank and such a shining past behind me and such a grand future ahead. That's why I'm so proud of myself, and that's why I can look the world in the face and say that I never did wrong. Yes, that's the reason. Because I was raised with love—love and plenty of money. That makes the perfect child, and the child is father of the man, as that wise poet said."

Tom Willow stared. "Why, lookit, Mr. Litton," said he, "you ain't as bad as all that. Why—your folks still living?"

"No," said Barry Litton. "They're not alive, thank God! They died—but not quite in time—not quite in time! Some of the truth about their darling came drifting back to them."

He walked into the front room, sat down, and shook out a newspaper. Tom Willow looked with perfectly round eyes at the boy, then he laid a finger on his lips.

"Never but once in my blasted life have I seen him

79

like this," he whispered. "Not even when them Malay swine run us off the deck and closed the hatches down on us. I wonder if—"

Jimmy glanced through the open door towards the bowed head of his friend, and tears suddenly stung the boy's eyes. He had loved big Blue Barry before, when he thought him a dauntless and a flawless hero. And now that his weaknesses were revealed, suddenly he knew that he loved him all the more. He must be helped. The very soul of Jimmy ached with desire to devise some useful scheme. But what could he do? What was his strength in such a crisis as this?

Supper was ready presently, before even a single idea had come to the boy. He prepared himself to sit through a dreary meal of silence and mere eating.

But he was wrong. Barry Litton had never been more entertaining. When they came to coffee, he sang Kanaka songs; and Tom Willow, enchanted by the half-forgotten melodies, beat time with his fist on his knee, and boomed out the few words he could remember in a voice like the husky roar of a sea lion.

"You've picked up spirits a whole pile during dinner," ventured Tom. "Jim, go give the chief some more coffee."

Jimmy was a flash of lightning, disappearing from the table, and appearing again with the coffee pot in his hand.

Wistfully he glanced at Barry Litton's face as the cup was filled. For Barry was still pale, and the lines in which it was set were more natural.

"I'm happier," said Barry Litton, "because I'm not thinking about home any longer. Home is a bad thing to think about, Tom, except for the good man. You understand?"

"Hey, and what's the matter with you, Barry?" asked Tom Willow. "A gent that never said no when a beggar or a friend stuck out a hand for help—a gent that never dodged trouble that he oughta face—"

"You stop there, Tom, and you'll please me a lot," said Barry Litton. His voice was so strange that Tom Willow was silenced far more effectively than he would have been by a direct command.

Jimmy's heart turned to ice.

Immediately afterward, the songs began once more,

and then Jimmy watched the pair of them, smoking and singing and laughing, and was sure that no trouble in the world could amount to much.

He had barely reached that conclusion, however, when Barry Litton rose, lighted a lantern that hung on the wall, and then placed it on a table between the stove and the kitchen sink.

"Hey, what's the idea of that?" asked Tom Willow.

"Just testing out a little theory of mine," said Barry Litton, gravely. And then he pulled out the drawn window shade, and let it fall over the lantern, shutting the lantern light out of the room, but letting it shine its message through the window pane!

14. A DEMAND

JIMMY LOOKED AT THE CLOCK THAT HUNG FROM A NAIL IN the wall. It was but a few minutes after eight. The message for Rann Duval had been prepared well before the vital hour. Scorn and rage mixed in the soul of Jimmy Raeburn. And still he pondered, desperately. Something had to be done.

He remembered, suddenly, a maxim which Tom Willow was fond of using: "There ain't anything so bad that it can't be helped.—All you gotta have is brains and two hands." Jimmy had two hands, but what was his brain worth?

There sat the great Barry Litton, the idol of Holy Creek, by far the greatest shining star that had ever moved across Jimmy Raeburn's horizon—and yet he was to sink, and be forever lost to view.

The boy knew perfectly that a man once humbled is never the same again. The defeated champion instantly becomes a third-rater. A man is mostly spirit, and when the spirit is gone, the flesh avails nothing.

Something had to be done! But what? If he had all the

powers of an army how could he help Barry Litton? To remove the obstacle from his path would not be of much help; because already the man had surrendered. All the more shameful—if he had surrendered to the dead! What means exist in this world for lifting the spirit that has once been cast down?

So, desperately reaching inside his mind, Jimmy remembered something that he had heard long before. He jumped up from the table.

"I forgot!" he exclaimed. "I gotta be going. Good night, chief. Good night, Tom."

"Yeah, you always remember something just when it comes time to do the dishes," said Tom Willow sourly. "Hey, wait a minute. I'm gonna tell you—"

But Jimmy was already through the door. He was running at top speed all the way back to his father's house. He was staggering and gasping by the time he got there. It would not do to enter the house in such a condition, so he threw himself flat on the ground and closed his eyes, dragging in great, regular breaths, as though he was sleeping, until his lungs stopped burning.

Then he got up. It was ten minutes past eight when he left the shack; it was a quarter past, now. Time was short —hideously short. At nine o'clock that deadly fellow, Duval, would walk past the shack and see the lamp burning in the window; and the small, chilly smile would touch his lips as he saw the sign of surrender.

Only forty-five minutes to avert that—and yet Jimmy dared not let the need of haste be shown.

He heard the rattling of dishes. His father liked an early supper, and now his sister was doing the dishes. As he passed the side window of the parlor he could see his father stretched in his easy chair, his slippers on his feet, in his shirt-sleeves, with his spectacles far down on his nose. For the first time, Jimmy looked into that face with understanding of the fingermarks which life had left upon it.

He paused one second to note all this, soberly. "I've growed up," said Jimmy Raeburn to himself. "I've growed up, and there ain't anything that hurts so much."

At the kitchen window, he looked in on his sister. Lou had finished the dishes, and she was now working on the pans, and he could hear the grating of the sandstone against the metal. He opened the back door and stepped inside.

"Hello, Jim," said she, without turning. "Take a towel and dry those dishes, will you?"

"Lou," said he, "d'you believe in me?"

She lifted her head, without turning it. Then she laughed softly. It had never occurred to Jimmy, before this night, that Lou's laughter was a very musical sound. He had always looked upon her as one of the most insignificant creatures in the world—just a girl! But now she was the only engine with which he could hope to accomplish a great purpose. She seemed to him insufficient, but she was the best that could be found.

"What's coming now, Jim?" said his sister. "Don't you want to wipe the dishes for me? You don't have to. I believe in you that much—I believe you're tired enough to go to bed. You always are, after a day with Barry Litton."

"Him!" said the boy. "It's about him!"

His voice plucked at her like a hand. She whirled about.

"What's the matter, Jimmy?" she demanded.

He noticed that her voice was pitched low. It could not possibly reach to her father in the front room.

"I'm gonna try to tell you, Lou," he said. "I ain't got no time, but I'm gonna try to tell you."

She went to him and took him by the arm. "You're trembling, Jim," she said.

She put a hand on his forehead and pushed back his face so that she could look straight into his eyes. "Now, what's the matter, honey?" said she.

"You gotta do something for me," said the boy.

"I'll do anything in the world for you, Jimmy," she said. She smiled a little, but he recognized her deep seriousness, and blessed her for it.

"I'm gonna ask you to do something," said he, "and you're gonna do it.—My God, there ain't much time! You're gonna do it, and you ain't gonna ask any questions. Just do it!"

"Yes," she said instantly. "Stop trembling, Jim. I'll do anything I can—anything that's right."

"It's right," said he. "There was never nothing so right. You roll down your sleeves and go straight back with me to Barry's shack. I wait outside; you walk in. You say to Barry Litton, 'Where's Jimmy? We expected him back before this!' Just something like that, you are to say to him. You understand?"

"I don't understand at all," said she.

"Go say it, then, without understanding!" he insisted.

"You'll have to tell me first—" she began; but then she was silent before the desperation in his face.

"He'll say that I just left a few minutes ago," the boy went on hurriedly. "You say that I'll turn up, all right. Then say something more. Before you go, say that you and father know I'm all right when I'm with Barry Litton.—Would you say that?"

Still searching his face, she nodded.

"And when you say it," said the boy, sweat bursting out all over his face, "could you smile at him, Lou?"

She caught her breath. "Jimmy," exclaimed his sister, "what *are* you driving at?"

"Could you say," he pleaded, "what I've *heard* you say—that he's the bravest man you ever knew? Would you say that?"

"I can't flatter him to his face!" she protested.

He caught hold of her hands and pressed them together. "Suppose he was sick, and that he was worse than dyin'. Suppose that speaking a few words would give him a lift and save him?—Would you do it then?"

"Yes," she said, "but—"

"Don't say 'but'!" exclaimed the boy earnestly. "I tell you, he's up and walking about. But I'd rather see him in bed, and the doctor telling him that he's going to die! I'd a lot rather! I'd a lot rather see him *dead* than to see him the way he is!"

His eyes were starting from his head as he added, "There's no time for thinking it all out!—You'll go or you won't go, Lou? Look me straight in the eye.—I tell you nothing but good will come of it. Will you trust me? Will you go?"

She rubbed her hands on a towel, rolled down her sleeves and hurried through the back door.

"I'll risk being laughed at for you, Jimmy," she said.

15. A WOMAN'S SMILE

JIMMY THOUGHT THAT ON THE WAY HE WOULD BE ABLE to explain more fully, but explanations did not come to him easily. And she, strange to say, asked no questions that might have brought words to him. But she went on with him cheerfully, until they were close to the shack which had once been Si Turner's, and he could see from it the light that shone from the kitchen window like a fatal star.

He halted, ten steps from the door. "You go on alone. I'm waiting out here. Lou, I'd die for you, after this!" he told her in a whisper.

She pressed his hand and went straight on.

He was so dazed with the thing that he had ventured upon that he sank down on one knee and looked after her, and it seemed to him that rays and sparkles of light emanated from her, though of course that was merely a trick of his excited mind.

He could only turn over and over in his mind the thought that had swept through him as he sat despairing, not many minutes before, in a room of this same house. The thought was not original with him. It was a sentence out of a copy book. For certain bad behavior—namely, the too accurate shooting of paper twists with a powerful rubber sling—he had been compelled to remain after school and copy the sentence one hundred times. Six sheets of paper he had filled, from top to bottom, with the detestable words: "The smile of a woman makes a man tenfold a man."

It seemed idiocy. But people who write copy books are supposed to know. Besides, he had seen pretty women turn grown men into gibbering idiots. If they had such power for evil, might they not have equal power for good?

There was one dreadful lack, of course; Lou was only his sister, and a mere girl.

Perhaps, he told himself as he dragged himself cautiously closer and closer to the house—perhaps she would do better than he expected. One always values home products cheaply. There was his old dog, Tiger, for whom he had felt only pity and contempt when the new dog of the village challenged Tiger in the open street, in the merciless glare of noontide, with twenty other boys in sight! But had not Tiger suddenly become worthy of his name, and in the end had not the other dog fled, howling?

It might be that Lou would rise to such a height.

But his heart fell into his boots when he saw Barry Litton's tall shadow meet her at the door, and saw her looking up with tilted head into the face of that fallen hero.

She merely said, "Hello, Barry.—Is Jim still over here?"

"No, he scampered off a few minutes ago," said Barry Litton.

"Oh, all right, then," said she, and turned away.

The scalp of the boy contracted and prickled with cold. Was that all? Was there to be no more? Oh, he that puts his faith in women—to say nothing of girls—

She reached the top of the steps. Barry Litton followed her; and the boy could see his wide, capable shoulders outlined against the stars of the night.

"Worried about Jim?" asked Barry Litton.

"No," she said, "not a great deal. Only—he was told to come home early. It's nothing. He's gadding about, somewhere. I don't suppose he'll come to any harm."

"I'll help you look for him," said the big man. He joined the girl at the head of the steps.

"Don't bother," she said, carelessly. "It's nothing, I'm sure."

Jimmy's very heart contracted with a silent groan. "The smile of a woman makes a man tenfold a man!" ran through his mind once more. Well, that might be true, but it didn't mean the smile of a slip of a girl who shrugged her shoulders as she spoke. Lou had meant well. The trouble simply was that she was only a girl. He should have found a woman; a woman who knew how to smile!

He heard Litton saying, "I owe apologies to you and

your father for the way I've monopolized Jim. I know you've been missing him a lot. But over here, we hardly know how to get on without him."

"Speak for yourself, will you?" roared Tom Willow's bass voice. "I'm gonna say that the galley of this here ship could be run a lot better without ever a sight of him around!"

Anger stirred Jimmy.

"Tom doesn't mean it," said Litton. "He's fond of Jim. So am I. And I've been keeping him to myself."

"He's a funny little mick," said Lou.

Surprise and rage boiled up in Jimmy. He was a "mick," was he?

"And we're glad to have him with you," Lou said. "We're both glad—Father and I."

"Are you?" said Barry Litton.

And as he spoke the boy saw him turn suddenly more squarely on Lou Raeburn.

"Father," she said, "believes in teaching by example."

"Not my example," said Barry Litton. "Don't say that!"

There was no smile on the girl's face. Bitterly Jimmy noted that. And had he not particularly asked her to smile? Otherwise, the whole thing was a lost venture. No, she was actually frowning in the dimness of the lamplight that came out about her face and shone in her hair.

"Why, what's the matter, Barry?" she asked.

"Nothing's the matter," he answered. "Only I can see the truth about myself, and the truth hurts worse than a sore tooth."

"You don't think you've set a good example for a boy?" she asked. "Is that what you mean?"

"Yes. I can tell you that," replied Barry Litton. "Even if I hated Jim, I wouldn't want him to be what I am."

She was silent for a moment. Still she did not smile. And Jimmy Raeburn, having given up all hope now, sat cross-legged on the ground, his chin on his fist.

Then she said, "You've done wild things, I suppose. But I know you're really brave and kind."

He answered, suddenly, "I can't talk any more about myself. I've been looking at myself only to-day, Lou, and it's a bad picture. Let's say no more about me. I can't stand it."

But she answered, "I'll say just one thing more. You're the bravest and the kindest man I've ever known.—I'll have to go back now," she added quickly, and turned down the steps.

Barry Litton reached the ground even before her, so that he managed to stop her, putting up his hand and touching her arm with it. And now, as he stood facing her, he was facing the light also, and dim though that light was, the boy could see the trouble in his friend's face.

"I won't stop you more than one second, Lou," said Barry. "I merely want to thank you for saying that much to me.—It happens to mean a lot to me, to-night.—You're blushing. You don't have to blush. You may give food to a starving man, some day, but it won't be of any greater value to him than what you've done for me to-night counts with me."

He stood back from her, and she hurried on down the steps.

"Good night, Lou!" he called to her.

She answered in a muffled voice which Jimmy could not turn into words; and as she went on into darkness, she stumbled once or twice. Big Barry Litton looked after her in a way that the boy could not understand, and then he turned and went slowly up the steps of the shack, his head hanging.

So that was all the interview was to mean?—that Lou went stumbling off into the darkness, and that Blue Barry went back up the steps of the house with his head down, like a beaten dog!

Jimmy jumped up and overtook Lou.

"You're going the wrong way, Lou," he said. "You're heading too far to the left. You'll be in the barbed wire in a minute."

She stopped, and her grip on his arm was like the grip of a man. "Why did you make me do it, Jimmy?" she gasped. "Oh, why did you make me do it? I've been a horrible, cheap, dreadful, silly fool!"

"Quit it!" said Jimmy, sternly. He had observed that sternness was always the thing with women. "Quit it and pick your head up, will you, Lou? Come on along, and quit blubbering like that! You're all right; you did your best.—You weren't old enough, that's all."

"Old enough for what?"

"Aw, nothing!" said he.

She caught him by the shoulder and shook him with amazing force.

"Jimmy Raeburn," she said through sobs, "what do you mean?"

He glanced over his shoulder at the light that still gleamed, farther away and more fatal than ever, from the kitchen window of the shack where Barry Litton lived.

"I don't mean nothing," sighed Jimmy. "Only, I hoped for something.—But you were too young. You didn't know enough. You didn't know how to talk."

"For what? How should I have talked?" she asked.

"Aw, Lou—what's the use?" said the boy. "If you'd been right, you would have made him ready to—"

He snapped his fingers. There was agony in his heart, but he knew that he must not confess to her the terrible tragedy that was about to take place—the most horrible of all things that may happen in this world, the shaming of a proud man!

Like a beaten dog, the great Blue Barry had gone back into the house; and a beaten dog he was—a shamefully beaten dog, ready to run. Sickness that was of both body and soul had come over him.

"I'll try to forget that I went," Lou was saying, dabbing at her eyes. "But, oh—"

"Oh what?" asked the boy, impatiently. "Nobody bit you, did they? You're all right, ain't you?"

He was surprised to hear her say, "Jimmy Raeburn, sometimes I wish—I wish that I could *beat* you!"

"Now, whacha mean by that, Lou?" he asked gloomily. "But don't you go and tell me, because I don't want to know. Right now, I'm thinking of something else that's a lot more important."

"More important than the way you've humiliated your sister?" she asked. She began to weep again.

"I didn't humiliate you none.—Aw, quit it, will you? I can't think," said Jimmy Raeburn.

He looked forward sadly into life. What would *he* do when the time came, and he had to face a Rann Duval? Even to think of the man was like thinking of some terrible poison!

A heavy sound struck on his ear, strangely close and

89

yet far away; a brazen booming that, as it died, he recognized as the first chime of the bell that stood in the clock tower of the city hall, the pride of the citizens of Holy Creek. And that chime was for nine o'clock!

It was a death knell on Jimmy's ear, and slowly turning he looked back at the little shack. The whole side of it was dark!

He caught Lou and jerked her about. "Lou, I ain't crazy, am I?" he gasped at her. "Is there any lamp shining out of a window, yonder, or ain't there?"

"Jimmy, are you out of your wits?" she demanded, still half sobbing. "Of course there's no light. You can see for yourself!"

It was true. The lamp had been withdrawn! Jimmy rarely showed emotion, but now he hurled himself on Lou and squeezed her with all the power of his strong young arms.

"Lou," he cried, "you've done it! You've won!—Lou, you're the best girl, and the finest sister a boy ever had!"

"Jimmy," said she, startled almost beyond words, "what on earth do you mean? What's got into you tonight?"

"I mean," he said, "that I'm gonna *slave* to make you happy the rest of my days, because you've done it. You won—even if you didn't smile."

"Smile? *What* do you mean?"

"It may be the finish," said Jimmy Raeburn, "but he's gonna die like a man, anyway."

16. PARTNERS

LOU SAID HARDLY ANOTHER WORD UNTIL THEY CAME back to the house. Their father's voice lifted, calling, "Hello, Lou!—Where are you?"

"I'm here," she said.

Samuel Raeburn came out on his veranda. "Where you been, honey?" he asked, with concern.

"I went to get Jimmy. He mustn't bother Barry and Tom all the time. They'll get tired of him."

"Jimmy, you're a gad-about," said the father, carelessly. "Well, I was just a little worried, that was all. I don't want you tearing around all over the place after dark, Lou. Remember that?"

"I'll remember," she said.

"I'm going to turn in," said Raeburn. "You youngsters be quiet, will you?" They went around to the kitchen door.

"I've got to go back," said Jimmy.

"Why?" asked the girl.

"I forgot something."

"You come in here with me a minute, Jimmy," said she.

He went inside with her, filled with a foreboding of trouble, and under the light of the kitchen she examined him carefully.

"You said something about Barry dying," she told him. "And you spoke as if you meant something by it, Jim. What did you mean?"

"Aw, nothing," said he.

"Do you mean that because of something that *I* did tonight," she said, still carefully studying him, "Barry Litton is to die—like a man?"

"Quit it, Lou," said the boy. "It's something that you wouldn't understand anything about!"

"I'll start in trying," said she.

"You wouldn't know about it, Lou," he told her, pleadingly. "I gotta go now."

"Back to Barry's place?"

"No, I've got to go over to the Standish house."

"What are you going to do there, at this time of night?"

"I forgot to tell Ed Standish something."

"What?"

"Quit it!" said he. "I don't have to tell you everything."

"No, you don't have to," she answered. "I didn't *have* to go with you to-night, either, when you begged me to go and play the fool!—You don't have to go to the Standish house; you're going back to Barry Litton. Jimmy, do

91

you really mean that he's going to die to-night?—Like a man, as you call it? Is that what you mean?"

"Look, Lou," said the boy. "What would I know about anything like that?"

"It means a lot to me, Jimmy," said his sister, simply.

He felt, suddenly, that she was no longer speaking to him as to a child. She was appealing to him as she would have to a grown man. He was amazed and moved.

"You like Barry?" he asked her, curiously.

"Yes, I like him. It wasn't on your account only that I was willing to go over there to-night."

"You like him a pretty lot?" he repeated, scratching his head in bewilderment.

"Yes, I like him a pretty lot," said she, and he thought he saw tears come into her eyes.

He was surprised. She was never one to give way foolishly to random tears. As a rule, she was more like a boy than a silly girl.

Finally, with a great effort, he said, "It's like this, Lou—You cross your heart to die?"

"I'll never say a word to a soul," she answered, eagerly.

"Not about nothing?"

She nodded. He considered this promise for a moment. To be sure, she was one who kept promises—she was not a tattler or a babbler—but after all, she was only a girl.

Finally he said, "It's a bad pinch with Barry, but he's come through the worst of it, all right—thanks to you."

She puckered her brow, but asked no foolish questions.

"There's still a rub to come," said Jimmy, cautiously. "I dunno how bad. That's why I wanta get back over there. Mind, you ain't saying a word?"

She suddenly looked away from him and through the open door of the kitchen, as though she saw something beyond the world.

Instantly, Jimmy slipped out that door.

But she did not protest. "No, I'm not saying a word," she replied, faintly. Still she did not see him, and her hands were folded against her breast as Jimmy saw the last of her.

He went hastily across the fields, saying to himself, "Lou has gone and sort of grown up, all at once! We both have."

A great deal that had happened on this night he was

unable to understand at all, and he felt that by some chance he had mingled elements that had turned to gold. He decided, finally, that Lou was quite a girl. There was something about her—She was almost as worth-while as an older brother!

When he got to Barry's shack, his eyes were probing the darkness in all directions, for might not skulking figures approach the little house—more especially that one small but terrible form of Rann Duval?

But when he ran up the back steps and entered the kitchen, he sang out, "Hope I'm not too late to help wash things up, Tom?"

Tom, with his sleeves rolled up above his tattooed forearms, looked over the edge of his newspaper and scowled at the small figure in the doorway. He tilted his pipe.

"Why," said he, with careful irony, "I guess you been hurrying to get back in time to do the dishes. Gonna break your heart, I guess, because they're done already, you lazy little vagabond of a roustabout, you!"

Some natural warmth came into the last words, but the boy cared nothing for it. His glance was for the dim form which he could see walking back and forth in the unlighted front room—vague glimpses of that form, as it swung across the doorway, and out of sight again.

Then Barry Litton called out, "Come here, Jimmy."

The boy hastened in to the big man, and a hand reached out and fell on his shoulder gently.

"Jim," said Barry Litton. "I'm going to say something that may seem strange to you. But I hope you'll understand. I don't want to hurt your feelings."

"Fire away!" said Jimmy. "We're partners, ain't we?"

"Right from the start!" agreed Litton, heartily.

"Well," said Jimmy, "partners always can talk out to each other, I guess."

"Thanks, Jim," said Litton. "It's like this.—For a few days I can't see you. I'll miss you. Nobody in town that I'd rather see. But just for a few days, I'm going to ask you not to come near this place—or me. No matter where you see me—keep away—never follow. Is that all right?"

Jimmy drew a great breath, and exhaled it as a sigh. "I guess you mean it for the best, Barry," said he, and he felt as though great, brassy doors were slamming in his face and shutting him into outer darkness.

93

Well he knew the meaning of this request.

Bullets were apt to fly now wherever Barry Litton appeared, and for that reason Jimmy had been asked not to come near him.

But because of that very danger, it seemed to Jimmy Raeburn that the one place in the world he wanted to be was at the side of his hero. For Barry Litton was a hero again—and to the boy he seemed ten times the hero, since that cold giant, Fear, had been mastered.

"I mean it for the best," he heard Barry Litton saying.

"Well, I'll go along home, then," murmured Jimmy. "So long for a while, Barry!" He put out his hand.

When Barry's friendly hand closed over his own, Jimmy gripped hard. He felt that he was saying farewell, and that never again would he touch that living hand—never again hear that voice.

"So long, Jim!" said the big man. "You're going straight home, are you?"

"Yeah, straight."

"That's the boy!" agreed Barry Litton. "I'll send you word when the coast's clear."

17. A ONE-MAN JOB

JIMMY RAEBURN, ONCE HE WAS IN THE OUTER DARKness of the night, blinked at it and shook his head. There was an odd choking feeling in his throat, and a sense of pain went straight through the center of his body. It was like being at a funeral, except that the dead man was still alive and walking.

So it was that he happened to stand for a long moment under the wall of the shack, and heard Barry Litton's voice carry clearly through the flimsy wall as he said, "Tom, pack your things."

"Well, doggone my eyes!" said Tom Willow. "I'm glad to be movin'. That Dead Man Steer has been on my nerves. I been dreamin' about it.—But I reckoned that it was about time for you to budge along. You've used up all the excitement in this here place."

"You think so?" murmured the big man.

"Sure. What's left to be done?"

"Well, anyway, pack your bag, Tom."

"It's packed already," said Tom Willow. "I ain't travelled with you so long that I don't pack my bag every day. When a gent travels with a hawk, he's got to keep ready to fly." He chuckled as he said it, and his chair grated heavily on the floor as he pushed it back under his weight, in rising. "What time we start, sir?" he asked.

"You start alone, Tom," said Barry Litton. "I stay here."

"Hey hold on!" exclaimed Tom Willow. "What's the idea of that?"

"I've got a one-man job here," answered Barry Litton. "Start fast, Tom. I want you away from me."

"I'm gonna hear why, I hope," said Willow with dignity. "Have I let you down, sir?"

"You, Tom? Never in the world! You've been the true steel, from first to last.—Wait a moment. You'll need some money to travel on. I've got nearly twenty thousand, here. You take fifteen of it."

Jimmy could actually hear the paper bills rustling, as they were counted out. He was staggered by the bigness of the sum which Barry had named. Were not whole ranches sold for less?

Then, like the bark of an angry dog, came Tom Willow's voice, "To hell with the money! I want facts! What's the matter, Mr. Litton?"

"The matter is, Tom," said Litton, "that I've come to a place where I have to paddle my own canoe. You take this money, shake hands with me, and forget me. Later on, you'll find out why. Just now, the thing for you to do is to leave me.—Do as I say, Tom. Take this money, and go. You've been the finest fellow in the world. But you can't help me now."

There was a loud sound of the clearing of a throat.

"I wouldn't even touch a dirty shaving off of a single dirty dollar!" said Tom Willow, emphatically. "Why, we've played a thousand close games together, you and me— and show me the tight place where two men ain't better than one? Tell me that, sir, will you? If it's from sailin' a ship to swabbin' down the decks, two men are better'n one every time—except where there's a woman in it."

"There's no woman in this, Tom," said Barry Litton.

"Now, doggone my eyes!" exclaimed Willow, "but I think there *is* a woman in it! Because you've had a funny look about you ever since the sister of that freckle-nosed brat come over here this evening! You've looked kind of different. Kind of wild in the eye. She's behind it!"

"I'm not sending you away because of her," said Barry Litton, evasively.

"A sneakin' little craft like her, even if she's clipper-built," said Tom Willow, "oughtn't to make no difference—"

"Be quiet, Tom!" said Litton's voice.

"Yeah—I'll be quiet. But I'm stayin' on with you, sir. I'll pipe down and shut my mouth, but I'll stay on."

"Then I'll have to tell you," said Barry Litton. "Stacey's on deck."

There was a pause. Jimmy, following it with bated breath, almost choked before he heard Willow's gasp: "Stacey?" he gasped, hoarsely. *"The* Stacey?"

"He's on my trail," said Barry Litton. "Grab your bag and go. He may be here this evening, for all I know!"

"Well, sir," said Tom Willow, "I ain't one to match a tramp freighter agin a passenger flyer. If it's Stacey—why, he ain't the meat for the likes of me to carve, I guess."

His hasty footfall sounded. He passed into the front room, and in a moment returned again; and all the while the aching sorrow increased in Jimmy Raeburn. It seemed to him that if there was a God, that God to whom some people prayed, He surely would not permit this man to be so stripped of all friends, and then given as a victim into the terrible hands of Stacey!

After a time, the dragging, noisy footfall of the sailor returned to the kitchen.

"I'm a worthless hound, sir," said he, miserably.

"You're simply a sensible man, Tom," said Barry Litton. "You know what Stacey is. He never fails—not twice with one man. I've beaten him once, but I'll never beat him again. The devil that helps him would never let that happen. Stacey's too fiendishly clever for ordinary crooks like me, Tom. He's too clever with his head—and with his hands. Besides, he'll kill from the dark, or from behind a bush. It doesn't matter to him. The killing is what he wants, and he always gets it."

"I know," said Tom Willow. "I'd only likely be something for you to trip over in the middle of things . . . Stacey!" he added, in a mutter.

Barry said, "Here's the money, Tom.—Good-by, old fellow. You've been true blue, all the way."

"I'm a sneakin' rat!" said the sailor. "But—I couldn't weather the typhoon, sir!"

"Of course you couldn't. I wouldn't want to have you here. Numbers don't matter against Stacey. And anyway, he'll probably have twenty picked thugs coming after my scalp. You'd simply be in the way, Tom. Good-by, and a thousand times, good luck to you! Let me give you one bit of advice: keep away from the booze. Go quiet for a year—and then perhaps you'll find that a quiet life will mean something to you."

"Good-by, sir," said Tom Willow. "I—I—" His footfall stamped hastily towards the door, then it passed on to the front veranda and down to the ground.

A feeling of bitter loneliness gathered around Jimmy Raeburn as he thought of the man left alone in the shack, when such terrible peril was collecting about that lone man.

Then a rush of clattering feet crashed up the front stairs, and the front door was burst open.

"Mr. Litton!" roared Willow.

"Ay, Tom?" called Litton.

"Look here, sir.—After sailin' in the kind of weather that you make, what would ordinary days mean to me, sir?—Stacey or no Stacey, here's where I stay. There's your damn money again—may the heart rot out of it for temptin' me!— And there's my bag, down to stay down. Also, here's me, sir; and if you want me out of the house, you'll have to throw me out!"

Jimmy could hear no more. There was a buzzing in his ears, and a sort of drunken joy that set a pulse to throbbing in his temples. He walked away from the house holding an uncertain course; but as he stumbled along, he was smiling. The world, after all, was not such a bad place! And for a devotion such as Tom Willow was showing, now, was not death itself almost a cheap price?

The boy came to the first fence. Pushing down the first wire with one hand, and raising the second with the other, he started to slide through, had put one leg on the ground on the opposite side.

It was while he was in this position that he saw a pair of skulking, stooped forms, stealing straight towards him. He could not have any doubt that he was their target, because they moved along lines that converged upon him, as a point.

With a faint cry, he tried to jump the rest of the way through the wires, but his hand slipped, and the upper wire, flicking strongly down, drove half-a-dozen barbs through his shirt and into his flesh. He squealed like a frightened little rabbit.

There was an answering cry from the pair pursuing him. He saw them lurch forward at a run. They looked big—they looked as big as ogres out of fairy tales—and with every stride they seemed to him to grow even larger.

He had one frightful moment of weakness, when he was sure that he was about to faint; then his head went crystal clear. Their hands were reaching for him when fear, like an anesthetic, made his pain disappear. He wrenched himself free from the wicked, crooked little barbs that gripped his body; then he bolted straight across the field.

As he ran, he could feel vast, winged shadows sweeping up into the sky to drop upon him. He turned his head a little, and saw the monstrous forms vaulting over the barrier. Then they were stretching their long legs after him.

It was a stubble field. He found the trail which had been made by the massive wheel of a harvester, then he sprinted down this fair track, wavering with the very effort. There was only one drawback—his shoes. Why had he not gone barefooted this day! With almost every step of the flattened straw that polished the ground he slipped a little.

Behind him he heard the beating of feet. He could almost feel the reaching hands. He did not need to see them.

He twitched his head about.—Yes, a long arm, a vast hand was extended towards him!

He planted both feet, twisted nearly double, and

dodged straight back. A fist struck him on the back and almost dashed him to the ground; but he managed to keep his balance during a few stumbling steps, and then he was racing back toward the fence that had almost snagged him before.

They were coming, cursing as they ran. But their weight and their velocity, and perhaps the surety they felt that the prize was theirs, somehow, made them lurch ahead before they turned, and so lose precious ground.

Who were they? Chaneys? Morgans? Fellows who had a desire to brush him out of the way so that they could get more easily at Barry Litton?—No, for this was Stacey's night, and so these must be his people.—Stacey, who loved to murder in cold blood! His men would stop at nothing.

What would the slaughter of a boy mean to them? A mere nothing.—They would throw the red rag of his body in the creek, with a stone tied around its skinny neck, and they would go on!

So Jimmy told himself as he ran. His breath was short. He could not breathe at all, in fact, because his heart was so swollen that it filled all the space inside his ribs. Its hammering drove out the precious air, and he felt himself to be choking.

He glanced back again. They were coming close, gaining with frightful rapidity. He ran as in a nightmare. His knees jerked straight up and down.

It seemed to him that he was making no progress at all. Then once more the dim skeleton of the fence rose suddenly before him.

He was unable to vault it; he could not dodge; there was no time to slip between the barbed wires. He could only fling himself on his back and try to slide under the lowest wire.

So he hurled himself down, feet first, like a sliding base-runner. A barb ripped through his shirt and scratched his breast, but that was nothing. That was only the touch of a spur that helped him to roll instantly to his feet; and as the two men vaulted the fence again, each with a panting curse, Jimmy sprinted down the side of the fence towards the creek.

18. A JACKRABBIT

JIMMY RAEBURN KNEW EVERY STEP OF THE WAY, for he was following the path to the swimming hole. It was not really a creek that flowed here, a mile out of town, but a mere trickle of water that gathered, in places, into shallow ponds. The boys of the village went racing there after school. Those races and most of all the slower homeward journey after the swim, when with loitering steps all the boys went sadly toward the close of day—when there were cows to be milked, wood to be chopped, scolding voices to be listened to—those races and the slow returns had fixed in the mind of Jimmy Raeburn every inch of the way. Now it seemed to him that the pale, distorted trunk of the old tree which had been struck by lightning spoke to him with a ghostly voice as he went by. "This is Jimmy Raeburn's last race.—This is the last of Jimmy Raeburn!" it said. The Twin Rocks, those black and ragged monsters which the more daring boys were wont to climb when playing tag, loomed right and left. It seemed to Jimmy that they stretched shadowy arms of protection over him, to shield him from the enemy in close pursuit.

But on the hard path the beat of the pursuing feet drew closer. And Jimmy was winded—terribly winded! One long breath, drawn deliberately to the bottom of the lungs instead of gasped hurriedly in and out, would have been worth more than ever was a deep draft of spring water to a desert-bound traveller.

There was the hollow stump in which he had hidden when the "gang" took after him that exciting evening. It seemed to throw a whisper after him, like the hiss of a snake: "This is the last of Jimmy !"

Then all was a blur, and out of the blur there came steadily on behind him the pounding of the feet, drawing ever nearer. They beat a terrible rhythm into his brain:

"Kill him!—Kill Jimmy Raeburn! Kill him!—Kill Jimmy Raeburn!"

He wanted to give up and throw himself on the ground, begging for mercy. He wanted to cry and shriek.—He would remind them that he was the only son of Samuel Raeburn, that the Law would pursue them. Besides, he never had meant any wrong.—As for Barry Litton, he never would go near that man again!

No, he remembered the cold, still face of Rann Duval! Like master, like men. Duval's followers would simply pick him up by the hair of the head, bend that head back and stop his scream and his life with one long, deep slash with a knife. Then he would lie for a moment on the ground, kicking around in a circle, trying for one more breath that never could be drawn . . .

"Now—get him—!" gasped a voice in his very ear.

He dropped flat to the ground, skidding as a hand gripped his shoulder. But the grip was broken, and as the pair lurched past him, he was up again.

Terrible fear took the place of strength. He went on wings. The dark brush loomed before him. He dodged just enough to keep the branches on either side from whipping his body. He heard the two men crashing behind him, cursing, snarling.

Before him appeared the dim oval of the second pool, the small one.

He knew that pool, and every drop of water in it. Without hesitating, he rushed straight on. A hand struck his shoulder from behind. With a deep moan of fear, he leaped from the high bank and shot down.

He had a glimpse of black branches rushing up across the stars. Like sparks those stars were—the sparks from a universe on fire. Then he crashed against the hard face of the water.

He went down like a plummet, bumped the bottom, started to rise again. His lungs were bursting, but he knew what he must do. Even starlight, shining on smooth water, makes every object that breaks the surface stand out clearly. And the instant his head appeared, those men would begin to shoot.

Therefore, he swam to keep from bobbing to the surface. He wanted to blow out all his breath in a single gasp

101

and then drag down a great, delicious draft of pure air. But he dared not.

Somewhere he had heard of soldiers who, coming to water in the midst of a long battle, rushed into it and drank, regardless of the bullets of the enemy that struck them down and sent their bodies slowly eddying down the stream, red stains spreading through the currents. Now he understood how they had thirsted for water, as he for air!

It was worse than the pangs of death to endure and yet he barely broke the surface with his pursed lips, let out a little air, drew in a little more. It did no good. He was only breathing in the upper part of his lungs; it was the lower part, in the center of his body, that was burning up. The fumes went up to his brain, and his soul seemed stifled.

He risked drawing one long breath; he nearly choked, letting it out slowly. But gradually he knew relief. In a day, or a week, it seemed, he might be drawing into his lungs all the delicious air that he needed!

Near him he saw a small projecting branch. He caught the stem beneath the water, and let his face come up under the shadow of the leaves. Now he could see and hear; and instantly breathing was easier. And to reinforce him came a wonderful sense of victory. He had not won the battle yet but he might win it before the night had ended.

The cold of the water soaked the fever out of his body. The night wind touched his face gently. What a friendliness there was about familiar things! How beautiful it was to live—merely to live—to breathe again without fear. In his daydreams, he had always imagined himself as a king and a conqueror. Now he changed all of that. He would be content with any small thing that gave peace and a chance to breathe! All work seemed easy—to stand in the heat and smoke of a blacksmith shop, swinging a twelve-pound sledge—that was nothing at all! He would make that an ideal, and try to grow up to it!

These things flowed suddenly through his mind, and were gone into the thin distance as he heard the voices speaking from the bank.

"Busted his neck on the bottom, likely," said one.

"I hope he did, the rat."

"But maybe he's a water rat, and right at home in a pool."

"Yeah? Has he got gills to breathe with?"

"He might of fetched under water and got to the bank. Maybe he's lyin' here right under our noses, gulpin' the air."

"Yeah, maybe. It's gonna be a while before *he* walks out at night, and a doggone long time before he goes hangin' around the house where that gent Litton is."

"But what made the chief want him taken off so bad?"

"Ah, he wanted him cooped up a coupla days, was all. He said that this kid had more pairs of eyes in his head than a house fly."

"Suppose he lays there with his neck broke?"

"Who'll know the difference? He just come down and jumped into the pool—and was out of luck."

"Jumped in with his clothes on?"

"You take a wild kid like that, he wouldn't think nothin' of takin' a swim with his clothes on, if he felt that way."

"There's our tracks comin' down here to the edge of the pool. They could tell we was running, and that his tracks was running ahead of ours, too."

"That don't matter."

"No? It would just about hang us, is all. People get all smoked up when they find out that a kid's been bumped off."

"Duval'll take care of all of that, all right."

"Yeah, maybe Duval will. I dunno."

"You'll know when you know *him!*"

"Look here," said the other, in an argumentative tone of voice.

"Yeah?"

"If this Duval is as much as you say, why don't he take on Litton by himself, instead of bringin' in half a dozen others and makin' a murder out of it?"

"Lemme tell you why—because he plays sure. There ain't anything in the world that he's scared of—except makin' a fool of himself. But he plays sure. It ain't any fun to him to make mistakes. He never takes a chance when he can make a thing sure. That's why he keeps on winning."

"Well, maybe it's a good way."

"The sure way is always the good way."

"We better go back and tell him that the kid's drowned in the pool."

"Never tell him nothing that you ain't sure of. We can say that we *think* the kid's drowned, and that we *know* he's scared near to death. Run like a doggone little jack-rabbit, didn't he?"

"Yelped like a rabbit, too, when the barbs ripped into him."

"It'd make you yelp yourself, if they bit into you like they must of done to him."

"We better get back. They'll be waitin' for us, before they touch off the grass."

"Yeah, they'll be waitin'. Think of a gent like that Litton, that has a name for brains, settin' there in his house like a fool and lettin' himself be burned out! Think of that, will you?"

"I'd rather think it than be it!" said the other. "Let's get goin'. Kind of a game kid, wasn't he—this brat?"

"Yeah—too game. He got me all winded. About six times, I thought that I had him in my hand. He shifted every time, like a bird in the air."

Their voices receded; the bank shut them suddenly away to nothing.

And lying in the cold of the water, the boy began to shudder. He felt weak, and sick in body and heart. One thing was certain: he had done all that a boy—or a man—could be expected to do, on this night. Barry and Tom Willow would have to fight the rest of the battle for themselves.

19. ON THE SPIT

HE CLIMBED UP THE BANK ON HIS HANDS AND KNEES, for he felt too spent and shaking to walk upright, and as he struggled, he heard the chorus of the frogs begin again, a song that seemed to come out of the very ground before him, spreading out until it seemed to fill the world to the very horizons.

As he reached the top of the bank, he stood up and stretched himself, with a sigh. As he did so, the chime of the town bell floated with a deep boom to his ear.

"Blue!" said the first huge note to him, distinctly. And as the sound died slowly away, it seemed to dissolve into a murmured "Barry Litton! Barry Litton! *Blue* Barry Litton!"

What time was it? Midnight perhaps? For ages had certainly passed since, at nine o'clock, he turned and saw by the lightless window in the old Turner shack, that Barry Litton intended to die like a man.

But this was not dying like a man. To be caught in a burning house was to die like a trapped beast!

The bell struck again, *"Blue*—Barry Litton, Barry Litton!" And again and again that name seemed to mourn at his ears, *"Blue*—Barry Litton, Barry Litton!"

Ten times the bell chimed, and then there was silence, spreading and spreading, and the last whisper of the bell, as the sound died, was still, "Barry Litton! Barry Litton!"

There was good old Tom Willow, too, who had turned back to share the danger with his master. *He* was not one to flinch at the last hour. No, not even with fifteen thousand dollars in his pocket, and a free ticket of leave.

But Tom Willow had turned back to die when Barry Litton died. No ringing of a bell would ever trouble *his* conscience.

"I ain't old enough, or big enough," said the boy to his soul. "It ain't right, things like this all being heaped onto me. I've done enough. You take any other boy in town— would he do what I've done? I reckon he wouldn't. Not one of 'em."

He started straight toward his father's house, and then another thought stopped him. It was to be with fire. They were to burn Barry out, and Tom Willow. He could see the picture—Barry Litton springing gallantly from the flames, a revolver speaking from each hand as he rushed toward the enemy. But he would fall, riddled with bullets—and poor Tom Willow would go down beside him.

Jimmy whirled about to face his duty, and instantly his heart leaped. Death is not such a tall giant, when we face it honestly. At least, so Jimmy Raeburn felt.

He sprang into full speed, instantly, running towards the shack which Barry Litton and Tom Willow lived in. To be sure, the pair who had hunted him had a considerable start, but they had gone off slowly, and he could more than make up for that lost time, perhaps, if he ran with all his might.

The wind was from the west, from the direction of the town. They would therefore be ready to put fire to the grass along that part of the place. In fact, the grass grew highest in the small field, there. There was sufficient wind to carry the blaze at a gallop, throw a huge yellow wave of fire upon the little shack. It would go up like a match box!

So Duval would have a pair of men, perhaps, there to the west. But he and the rest of his outfit would take the other side, no doubt, to be the net in which the hunted would be caught as they fled from the fire!

Jimmy could see the thing clearly. It was really a strange thing that more people were not burned out. It was such a sure and simple way of committing murder without danger to the murderer.

He ran at top speed all the way to the shed behind Si Turner's shack. He had made up his mind, now, about the scheme he would attempt to use in entering the house to give his warning. The risk of it?—Well, he knew that if he paused one instant from violent action, fear would freeze him to the roots of the soul forever!

He saw nothing at all around the house, as he drew near. He came up behind the shed, both doors of which were kept open for the sake of giving more air to the mare inside. His own little mustang was kept beside the tall mare, for he had taken up almost permanent quarters with the great Barry Litton.

To that mustang he glided now, and prevented it from giving the usual whinny of recognition by pinching its nostrils hard. Instead of whinnying, it snorted and stamped, and to Jimmy Raeburn the sound was like the falling of a mountain.

He waited. Not a sound approached him. Duval's men had taken it for granted, perhaps, that hay dust had gone up the nostrils of one of the horses. That often happened, as they would know.

He found himself holding his own breath, as he had

done under the water of the pool—his eyes began to ache in the same way. Now, breathing again, he slipped the headstall of the halter from the mustang and backed it gradually out of the wings of the stall.

They were old companions, he and that little bundle of fiery energy, and this was but one of the tricks that they had so often played together, when Jimmy was conducting mimic Indian wars.

Slipping off the shoes that had so nearly been his undoing, he swung onto the back of the little horse, and lying over, hooked the bend of his elbow just forward of the withers, where a fine growth of mane fluffed over the arm and fairly concealed it.

That was his right arm. His right leg he slid well back, and hooked the instep over the loins of the horse. In that way, he was suspended along the side of the mustang, in a position that he could quite easily have kept for some time, had there been a saddle to assist. As it was, his foot was continually in danger of slipping from the smoothly rounded back of the pony.

He had his left arm stretched out along the neck of the horse—a pressure to one side, a pull against the mane, would turn it in either direction he wanted. And now, with a nudge, he started the animal toward the open door of the shed and the house beyond.

His hope was that, since none of him showed against the sky, except an almost invisible heel, projecting above the back of the horse, he might escape detection—unless they suspected the movements of the horse, and came to inspect more closely.

Out through the door of the shed they moved, and suddenly a low voice muttered, on the far side of the horse, "Hold on! What the devil is that?"

"Aw," muttered another, "it's the kid's mustang. It goes around the place like a dog."

Straight on went the little pony. Halfway to the house it paused, put down its head, and wrenched at a tuft of grass. Jimmy nearly fell to the ground. He was hanging merely by a toe, and it seemed certain to him that he was falling. If that happened?—Well, the dark of the night would blossom with gunfire, of course! And his body would be riddled!

Another voice, not far behind him, said, with strange clearness: "How did that horse get loose?"

Jimmy knew that it was Rann Duval speaking.

Some one else answered in a murmur that the mustang was free most of the time, that it wandered about the place like a dog. That was true—a blessed truth for Jimmy!

He nudged the pony on. It went a few paces and stopped for another bunch of grass! It was now a certainty that Jimmy could not remain on the back of the little horse another moment . . . His leg was shuddering clear up to the hip with the last of its strength, but he dared not renew its grip, dared not make any movement.

Three or four dreadful seconds, and then the pony went on again, and this time briskly, with a shake of its head, and a snort. That shake of the head was very nearly the finishing touch for Jimmy Raeburn!

All at once he was near the dark wall of the house. A whisper stopped the mustang just beside one of the low-silled kitchen windows. It was open. Jimmy could thank heaven for that. Cautiously, he swung his free leg over sill, then the rest of him glided in, snake-like.

He lowered himself softly to the floor. If the speaking of a single word could have saved a million lives, he could not have uttered it at that moment. When he rose, it was only to his hands and knees. On them, he crawled to the door of the front room.

Were they both asleep? Had they actually dared, on this night of nights, to go to bed and sleep? Jimmy had a hysterical impulse to break into laughter.

He had to gasp to control himself, and it was that gasp which brought Barry Litton's calm voice, saying: "Whoever you are, freeze on that spot, brother. I've got you covered, and ready for salting!"

"Barry!" whispered the boy.

"Damnation!" muttered Barry Litton. His step crossed the floor. He picked Jimmy up by the nape of the neck.

"You little fool—!" he said.

"Hush!" breathed Jimmy. "They'll sure hear you. They're outside—Duval and six more, and they're gonna light the grass to the west.—They're gonna burn you out. Barry, do something *quick!*"

In the darkness, Tom Willow cleared his throat, softly.

"I kind of might of expected that," he said. "I been roasting such a lot of birds all my life, that it's only kind of fair that I should get done to a brown turn myself, in the wind-up!"

Jimmy heard him actually chuckling at his own grim, whispered joke!

20. NOT THEIR NIGHT

SOMETIMES THE OPENING OF A SMALL DOOR GIVES UPON a great vista, and so it was now that Jimmy, through that murmured jest of Tom Willow, suddenly saw deeper than ever before into the natures of his new friends. He knew that danger had rubbed elbows with them ten thousand times before.

Blue Barry Litton merely said, "Jim, you're all gold! Say everything in ten seconds."

"They're gonna burn it from the town side. The wind's that way," said Jimmy. "There's a couple of 'em back at the shed. I came outa the shed stuck on the side of my horse, and they didn't spot me. I slid through the window, and that's all!"

"It's enough," said Barry Litton. "Tom," he added, "we're going to rush the shed. There's a pair of shotguns. Take one. They're loaded for bear. They'll reach anything near the shed. They're the only thing for finding a mark in the darkness.—I'm going first. You come through the door behind me. Jim, you come last. You're the rear guard. That's the most honorable position, you know. Tom, shoot at everything that moves. I'll keep the front door of the shed. Jim, you dive for the hay in a manger and stay there. Now move, everybody!"

He spoke so quietly, so gently, with such calm assurance, that Jimmy suddenly felt as though they were already in the horse shed.

Back into the kitchen they moved. He saw the two

men pick the shotguns from the nails that supported them on the wall. Then big Blue Barry stood at the door.

Jimmy looked out the second kitchen window, and saw clearly, even by the starlight, the posts of the corral, where the Dead Man Steer was kept. An awkward looking shadow lay close to the ground.—That would be the steer itself. How many more would be killed in its name, tonight?

Jimmy looked out the other window in time to see a small, bright spot appear a hundred feet from the house, in the western lot, among the tall grasses.

"Quick, Barry!" he gasped. "They're firin' the grass."

He could see two dim forms leaning above two bright spots. The fire dwindled, and then leaped up again.

"Come!" said Barry, and that instant he thrust open the door.

Before it could close again, Tom Willow leaped out behind his master. Swiftly the boy followed, catching the screen door on the rebound and shutting it noiselessly.

Silently they ran on, in stockinged feet.

"Hey!" yelled a wild voice. "They're comin'—there's *three* of 'em!"

A blast of fire and a roar came from Blue Barry's gun, carried low at the ready as he sprinted forward. A screech answered the shot. Jimmy saw a shadow leap up at the corner of the horse shed, double over like a jack-knife, and fall with a thud.

Then guns opened with a rapid chatter, left and right. A wasp stung Jimmy Raeburn on the end of the nose, and brought such tears into his eyes that he went half blind and collided with the edge of the sliding door as he made the final leap for the shelter of the horse shed.

Still the guns were barking, like rapid thunder. Bullets crashed through the flimsy walls, and he flung himself on the ground.

"Jimmy," breathed Barry Litton's voice, close behind him, "are you hurt, old son? Did they get you?"

"Not me, Barry," said the boy, blinking the tears out of his eyes. "What about you?" he added, with a hot rush of pride in this companionship in danger.

"I'm not even scratched. And Tom's all right, to judge by the talk of him."

110

For as fast as he could, Tom Willow was loading and firing the big shotgun he carried.

The answering fire outside the shed suddenly stopped.

"Bill," called a clear, quiet voice, "are you fit to ride, if I come for you?"

That, as the boy knew, was the voice of Rann Duval.

Near the shed a groan answered. "Leave me be. I've got enough lead to keep me the rest of my life. Go on and take care of yourselves, all of you. It ain't our night!"

Instantly, hoofbeats began; and jumping up and peering out through the door of the shed, Jimmy Raeburn saw horsemen flashing out of sight in the distance.

There was plenty of light to see them by now, for the fire, exactly as he had known it would do, had taken only a moment to gather a head. It now rolled up in one brilliant, golden billow that broke upon and overwhelmed the house. With that final stroke of disaster, Jimmy Raeburn knew that the perils of the night had ended.

He turned, instinctively, and looked towards the corral, where the Dead Man Steer had lurched to its feet, and now stood bellowing a long and dismal note, its head thrust out and its back arched. It almost seemed that the animal had expected blood, this night, and had not found enough.

But blood there was, in a horrible plenty, around the poor fellow who lay near the horse shed. He was a small man with a swarthy skin, and eyes black enough to be an Indian's or a Mexican's. He had a few scattering hairs on the upper lip that might have passed for a mustache, and his dark, heavy brows were contorted with pain.

They examined him hastily, after they had carried him back into the shelter of the shed. Three slugs had struck him, one tearing through the leg, another plunging into his body on the right side, and the third making a gory scalp wound.

Barry Litton looked after the wounds with a quick, sure hand. And as he worked, the roar of the fire outside told of the end of old Si Turner's shack.

The whole town came, with the shooting to waken it and the blaze to direct its attention.

Si Turner was among the rest, and leaning against a corner of the horse shed, close to the spot where Barry Litton was working over the wounded man, he said,

111

"Well, sir, now that she's gone, I gotta say that I'd rather of seen my big house go up in smoke."

"I'm going to pay for the place, Si," said Barry Litton, without looking up from his work.

The old man turned slowly, and blinked at the other. "Why, boy," said he, "what would you pay me for? That armful of dried old boards, maybe? Or would you pay me for the places where my hoofs wore grooves in the floor, walkin' around from the stove to the sink, and back again? Would you pay me for that spider, Mrs. Murder, who lived in one corner of the ceilin', Barry? Would you pay me for everything in there that used to remind me of old days? However, it ain't any matter. All things have gotta come to an end—houses and the men that live in 'em, too. Maybe I'm gonna find a hotter place than that shack is right now, before the wind-up!"

The doctor came and took charge of the wounded man, who from the first had given no token of pain. The only words he spoke were to Litton, as the latter gave over his work into the hands of the medical man. He merely said then, "You're white, son!"

The man himself was not old, but all men, even boys, are as old as time when they come close to death.

The man might not die; he might live, said the doctor. At any rate, he would have to be kept there on the floor of the shed, and on as comfortable a bed as could be made for him. It would be too great a risk to move him.

The sheriff was among the first of those present; and gathering a posse from the mounted men at hand, he rushed them off in hope of discovering the trail of the fugitives from justice while it was yet hot.

So, in the end, Jimmy Raeburn went home, hand in hand with his father, and with Lou.

Tom Willow said to Raeburn, "The kid saved us. Me and Barry Litton, we'd be the most doggone toasted saints in heaven, by this time, Raeburn, if it hadn't been for that lad yonder! He ain't much use around a house. But I've noticed that a handy man around the house ain't worth a rap outside it—excepting he's a sailor!" he could not help adding.

Barry Litton said nothing at all—not a word of gratitude. He merely waved his hand and called out cheerfully, "See you in the morning, Jim."

Jimmy's father said, on the way home, "Don't you go and get a swelled head, now, out of this. And what's the matter with your nose, that you got your hand to it? "What's the blood from? Something hit you there?"

Jimmy could not resist saying, casually, "Yeah, a rifle bullet."

Both his father and his sister exclaimed, but he waved their concern aside.

"Aw, it's nothing—it's nothing," said Jimmy Raeburn. "What's just a graze?"

But he knew that he was a made man in the house—for a week at least. Never could his eminence endure in his own home for more than a few days, unfortunately.

He had a single moment with Lou, before he went to bed. She washed the blood from his face, and put a white bandage across it, sticking it down against his cheeks with plaster. There were boys in that village who would give their heads for a similar distinction, when they saw his badge of honor the next day. Tired as he was, he could hardly wait for the morning to come.

When the bandaging was finished, she said, "Are you ever going to tell me the whole story, Jimmy—from the start?"

He thought of the graveyard scene and shuddered.

"You know how it is, Lou," he said. "You done a wonderful job to-night. You dunno why it was wonderful—and I can't tell you. But it was wonderful. Only, you know, Lou, there's some things that just gotta be left between men."

21. A POOR DEVIL—

WHEN BARRY LITTON AWAKENED THE NEXT MORNING he stared at the ceiling, then sat up in his blankets. Automatically, a figure sat up in a bed in the opposite corner of the shed. It was Tom Willow, blind with sleep.

"Lie down again, Tom," said Litton.

"Thanks, chief," said the sailor, and dropping back, he was instantly snoring once more.

At the pump, beside the corral, Litton bathed his face and shaved. It made little difference to him, the amount of time that he spent in bed. Like a camel able to go without water, so he with repose; the strength that was stored in him could be drawn out as from a tap, in the time of need.

As he shaved, he looked at the Dead Man Steer, contentedly lying there in the first light of the morning sun, the horrible brand on its flank swelling to a grin and contracting to a scowl with each deep, slow breath of the animal. Then he went back into the shed and squatted on his heels at the side of the wounded man.

A relay of nurses had watched him through the night. The grizzled cowpuncher who had the job at present was yawning hugely as Barry Litton appeared. Litton asked:

"How was the night?"

"There wasn't no night," said the cowboy dolefully. "There was only hell!—He ain't gonna last."

Said Barry Litton, "Who put you on this job, brother?"

"The doctor asked me," said the cowboy. "I dunno why he should of picked on me, though."

"You're relieved now," said Litton. "You go on and have a sleep. I'll take care of him."

The cowpuncher departed at once, and with joy.

Litton sat down beside the man he had shot, and laid his fingers on the other's pulse. It was low and fluttering. He looked into the man's face and noted the locked jaws and the enforced calm of the eyes.

"Let everything go, brother," said Litton. "You don't have to hold on so hard. You're wearing yourself out, fighting."

The other glanced at him in amazement.

"You're going to live," said Barry Litton.

"I'm not crying if I don't," said the other, hastily.

"Of course you're not! Only, I'll be telling you the facts. You can kill yourself just by keeping up the fight, by trying to be a tough fellow and a hero.

"You're a brave enough, partner. Only, don't hero it all over the lot. Just relax and take things easy."

The other stared more wide-eyed. "But ain't you Litton?" he asked.

"Yes, I'm Litton."

The stare continued.

"When you're back on your feet, we can start fighting again," said Barry Litton. "There'll be time enough for that. Just now your job is to keep your head up, and my job is to keep you from being a notch on my gun."

"Was it you that shot me, Litton?" asked the other.

"I did," said Litton. "I saw the flash of your gat as you fired from the corner of the shed, and I let you have it. I thought you were—somebody else!"

"Du—Yeah, somebody else!" said the other.

"Yes, Duval," said Litton.

"I didn't say nothing about Duval," said the wounded man.

"That's all right," said Litton. "We don't have to argue. You've never met Duval in your life, have you?"

"No, never."

"You're a good hearty liar, anyway," said Litton. "But I like a fellow who can lie. He's the one to trust in a pinch."

The other smiled, all on one side of his tense face.

"It's that grinding of the teeth that kills men," said Litton. "You'd better remember, old son!"

"Why?" said the other. "I'm not in any pain, much. I'm all right. I could use a cigarette, is all."

"Sure," said Litton. He passed over the wheat straw papers and the Bull Durham.

"You might roll one for me, if you don't mind, Litton," said the wounded man.

"Oh, you're able to roll your own, aren't you?" asked Litton.

"Why, yes, I can do that, too." He took the makings and made half a cigarette, when suddenly a twitch of his hands tore it in two. The second was ruined at the very start. The third was almost finished when a suppressed spasm caused him to tilt the little cylinder, so that the tobacco ran out.

"My fingers are all thumbs," said he. He proffered the makings back.

"Keep on trying," said Litton. "I can see you're not in any pain at all!"

The dark eyes rolled at him; there was no answer.

"Groan, brother," said Litton. "I wouldn't blame you.—But tell me where you hurt. Then I can start helping you."

Suddenly the sick man wilted. He seemed reduced, suddenly, to half his real dimensions.

"It's my side, Litton," he gasped. "I don't mind the pain—hardly. Only, it's the choking that comes afterwards—Oh, my God!" The last words grated from his throat in a deep groan.

"That's better!" said Litton. "Now you're relaxing. I'll have you fixed in five minutes, now—so comfortable that you'll go to sleep. Then one hour of good sleep will save your life."

He twisted a cigarette into shape with a single gesture of his fingers, placed it between the man's lips, and lighted it.

"Smoke that, while I get things ready," said he.

He picked up a bucket, filled it half full at the pump, went to the smoldering ash heaps of the house, kicked off the top coals, and settled the bucket in the red cinders.

While the water was heating, he went to the bed of hay that gave comfort to Tom Willow, and touched him. Tom opened one eye with a groan far louder than that of the wounded man.

"Tom," said Litton, softly, "this man yonder is sick with his wounds. Go get the doctor.—Get him by the nape of the neck, if you have to, and bring him here."

"I'll say that you sent me," said Tom, in the same sort of a hushed voice, as he rolled out of his blankets.

"Say that I sent for him. Say that I'm likely to come for him, too."

Barry went back to find the water already steaming; and taking the pail up, he carried it to the wounded man's side.

He unbuttoned the dirty, blood-stained shirt, and saw that the bandage around the body had been cinched with such great force that the skin below and above it was puffed out. Slowly, very gently, he slacked the bandage off.

A groan came from the very heart of the invalid. Sheer relief had brought the sound.

Litton pulled off his own shirt, dipped it into the hot water, and wringing it nearly dry, folded it as a compress, which he laid over the bandage, just above the wound.

Another groan welled up from the soul of the man. His eyes closed. "Thanks," he said. "God bless you!—God Almighty bless you!"

Suddenly he opened his eyes. "It seems to soak right in—right into the bone—the comfort of it, Litton." A brief smile twisted his lips. His eyes looked dull, now that the bright agony was passing from them.

"They told me that you were a low hound," said the wounded man.

"Steady, old son!" said Blue Barry.

"I'm going to sleep," said the other, drowsily. "Maybe I'll pass out while I'm asleep.—If I do, that's all right. But I'm gonna tell you a few things I know, before I kick out."

"Wait a minute," said Barry Litton. "You're feeling kindly, just now. But when you get on your feet again, you may wish that you were back with Duval, or some one like that. You don't owe me anything for taking a little care of you. When a man's up, he may be my friend, or he may be my enemy; but when a man's down, he's just a poor devil that needs help. He hasn't any past, as far as I'm concerned.—Now, you shut your eyes, and think that over. You'll be asleep before you finish the thinking, and you'll wake up almost well."

The other shook his head slightly, but he obediently closed his eyes; and almost at once, he began to moan softly, continuously. Barry knew that he was sleeping.

Only a moment later, the doctor came. Barry grinned when he saw how worried the doctor looked.

"What's the matter, Litton?" he demanded, as he hurried in. "Were you hurt last night, and didn't tell us anything about it?"

Barry Litton laid a friendly hand on the other's arm.

"Listen, doc," said he. "You're a good doctor, and you know your business. But last night you put the bandages on that fellow, yonder, in a pretty rough way."

"I can't be soft-handed with a murderous brute like that!" said the doctor grimly.

"Were you ever sick with bullet wounds?" said Litton.

117

"I?—Why, no!"

"Well, I've been sick with 'em—several times," said Litton. "Got any very important cases? Are there any patients you've *got* to see?"

"Business is pretty slack," said the doctor, naïvely. "I have a few little calls to make this morning, though—as soon as I'm through here. I've got to go over and see old man Hill—"

"Forget the calls," said Litton. "Let them go to the devil.—Your job is here, all day.—I'll pay for it. Just imagine that *you're* lying there, with the lead in you. Start working from that angle—and don't stop all day long!"

22. A CELEBRATION

A LAD CAME UP ON A RUNNING HORSE, AND PITCHED out of the saddle as he reached the door of the shed. He came to look at the wounded man, but Blue Barry turned him back.

"He's pretty sick," said Barry Litton. "Back up, and give him air for a while."

The boy jerked his shoulders.

"Here's something for you from the sheriff," he said. It was the briefest of notes:

DEAR BARRY:

Come quick, and come by the back way. I got to see you. You needn't make much noise.

Yours faithfully,
DICK WILSON.

Barry thanked the boy, slid a saddle on the mare, and cantered out of Holy Creek, turned behind the low hummocks to the right, then sped back down the side of the town, but hidden from it. In a close little grove of poplars, he left the horse, swung himself over a high board fence, and was in the back yard of the sheriff's house.

No one saw him enter the house. He stood in the kitchen for a moment, looking down at the linoleum. In the center of the room, and near the stove, it was worn to the cloth.

A shaft of strong sun struck through a window that had a cracked pane. Flies buzzed loudly in and out of that stream of powerful light, and little motes of dust wavered in it, all seeming to fly upwards. He looked from the worn floor and the shaft of light to the smokestained, cracked ceiling. Suddenly the world appeared to be a soiled and broken place.

He could hear voices sounding, toward the front of the house. He pushed up the kitchen window, and as the fresher air entered, and with it the noises of the outer world, he no longer felt as though he had entered a tomb. The feeling that all mortal existence was spent in a kind of grave left him.

He sat down by the window, but well back in the shadow, so that he could not be seen by people of the outer world. Then he made a cigarette and lighted it, breathing in the smoke deeply.

A heavy footfall came booming down the hall. He turned a little in the chair, and the sheriff stepped in on him.

The sheriff nodded curtly at Barry. "Kind of thought that you'd be in here," he said. "I got a coupla visitors in yonder that been askin' about you."

Narrowly Litton watched him. "Old friends of mine?" he asked.

"They seem to know a lot about you," said the sheriff. "They want me to pinch you, Barry."

"Do they?" asked Blue Barry. He breathed out a cloud of smoke, and then spread his fingers and looked at their tips with interest. "What do they want to run me in for?"

"Nothing much," answered the sheriff. "They want to get you for larceny, burglary, gambling, and half-a-dozen killings. Otherwise, they don't care whether they see you or not. They say there are some rewards on your head."

"Rewards?" asked Litton, innocently.

"Yes, rewards. They say that you're wanted in Malaysia, and in the Solomon Islands. They say that you're

119

wanted in Japan and in India, and that the doggone British Empire will pay a thousand or so pounds for you.—That always beats me, Barry."

"What? Putting prices on people, dead or alive?"

"Not that. That's pretty reasonable.—But calling money 'pounds.' There ain't any sense to it. What does a pound mean, anyway? It's a fool idea to call five dollars a pound!"

Litton shrugged his shoulders. "You want me to see your callers?" he asked.

"I want you here so they *can't* see you; and I don't want the fools to get loose and try to serve the warrants on you. I didn't want you to blow holes in 'em, Barry, so I sent for you here. Maybe it sounds kind of out of the ordinary, but I didn't know where they might look for you—except they never would dream of lookin' here, would they?"

"I hope not," said Barry Litton.

"All right, then. You stay here. If you want to, you can slip into the next room, and listen to their talk. They're talkin' pretty big. They're gonna get rich and famous out of you, boy."

"That's all right," said Barry Litton. "Go back in there and entertain them, and I'll slide back to the Turner place and wait. I don't want to hide in a hole, here. You'd be thrown out of a job if people knew that you shielded me from warrant servers."

"Thrown out of a job?" said the sheriff. Then he laughed. "Lemme tell you, boy, that all I've done is to drop a word to the lad that brought my note to you, and that kid is now busy spreadin' the news through Holy Creek that a pair of headhunters is out here, lookin' for your scalp. I dunno—but I think that some pretty funny things are gonna happen, before long."

He added, "I'll go back and chatter to 'em. You fetch into the next room, where you can hear—or just leave this door open.—They don't whisper none."

That much was true. In the next few moments, as he sat near the open kitchen door, Barry Litton learned that Mr. Jones, of the bass voice, and Mr. Tim Craven, of the nasal squeak, were building up a reputation as man-catchers. They hoped, one day, that their repute would go far and wide. The country needed a few expert man-catchers, they declared. They were ready to fill the bill. They were not only willing; fortune had also smiled upon them. In the meantime, they wondered if the sheriff would be able to lure the man to the house?

"Yeah, I might," said the sheriff. "He might come if I asked him."

"There's considerable of a crowd out there, gatherin' in the street and hangin' around," said Man-catcher Lee Jones. "Wonder what about?"

Said the sheriff, "In the old days, I used to spend a whole lot of time wondering about the way crowds got together in this town. But I've got over it. This here town of Holy Creek would furnish a crowd for a flea-jumping contest, I can tell you! A crowd'll gather in Holy Creek to watch a buzzard circle, or a hawk sail. And sometimes, they don't gather for no reason at all; but they just stand around and wait for things to happen. They think the main street is a sort of a show place, and doggone me if they ain't almost right.

"Now, I tell you what you boys could do.—You could go right out and appeal to that crowd, and tell 'em that in the name of the law, you'd like to have some help in the roundin' up of that Barry Litton. Just name the charges that you got against him, and the number of countries that want him, and I reckon that you'll raise a lot of excitement, right away quick!"

It was a great idea. Craven and Jones leaped at it. They said the scheme was made to order for them, and in half a minute they were standing out on the steps of the sheriff's house. The sheriff had not offered to accompany them. He said he wouldn't dream of claiming a share in the reward. They could have both the glory and the money to themselves—though he would introduce them to the crowd.

He did so, from the front porch of his house, while Barry Litton, from an adjacent window, looked on with a gleaming eye. Barry saw the pair of man-catchers, at last, Jones, a little dark-faced bulldog, and Craven, the long, lean, ever-hungry Yankee type. Happy anticipation brightened them, now.

The crowd in the street, at sight of the two—even before the sheriff spoke—began to drift in the direction of the house. It gathered instantly in a compact mob of men at

121

the foot of the steps, before the sheriff had spoken twenty words.

Those words were as follows:

"Neighbors, here's Mr. Craven, and here's Mr. Lee Jones. These two gents have come a long ways for the sake of doin' the law a good turn. They tell me there's a lot of countries that want Blue Barry Litton, the gent who's been living here in charge of the Dead Man Steer, lately. There's a pile of money to be made out of turning Blue Barry over to the law, and they've come a long ways on the trail of him. They aim to take in a pile of money for rewards, once they've got him; and since they've gone and worked so hard, I dunno that I'm likely to cut in on their reward money . . .

"But I told 'em that all you boys might be terrible interested in what they wanta do, and that you might take a hand in the job, one way or another.—Now, this here is a terrible busy day with me, gents, and I'm gonna go back in the house to write up some reports on how mean Holy Creek is. *Adios!*"

He turned to the two man-catchers and said loudly, "Gents, I wish you all the luck that's comin' to you!"

Then he walked back inside the house and was instantly at Barry Litton's shoulder.

The crowd, in the meantime, gave out a hoarse murmur that would have been hard to reduce to words, and it surged forward onto the steps. Craven and Jones saw the movement with obvious pleasure. Now big Samuel Raeburn stepped from the rest and mounted swiftly halfway up the stairs. There he turned. "Gents," he said, "it looks like this here is a business where we gotta take a hand, don't it?"

In answer, a tremendous and wild roar of yells and cheers answered him. The response first amazed, and then pleased, the two man-catchers.

Samuel Raeburn continued: "I guess every man in Holy Creek is pretty interested in law and order, eh?"

Another shout greeted his words.

He then said, "We want to show Jones and Craven just where we stand when gentlemen like them come around to clean up our back yards, so to speak, and so I'm going to ask them what they'd like to have us do to Barry Litton."

He got his answer from Craven, who said, "Boys, we take this mighty kind. There ain't any doubt that the citizens in a town oughta be interested in holding up the law, and when a mean man comes their way, they ought to show how they feel.—If I was you, I know how I'd feel. I'd wanta take that Barry Litton and throw him into handcuffs—we've got three pair with us, by the way!—and then I'd wanta tear the clothes right off of him, and roll him in tar and feathers, and ride him as far as the train on a rail. There I'd throw him onto a platform and tell him to go to the devil. Me and Jones, here, can sure promise you that we'll take him there!"

Samuel Raeburn turned and made an expansive gesture. "Gents," he said, "I guess that's all we wanta know. Jones and Craven have told us just what to do."

A frantic yell of joy from the many throats answered him, and up the steps flowed a torrent of men who caught up Jones and Craven and bore them off.

Cries of fear began to rise; but the shouting of the crowd, as it poured forward to a goal that seemed to have been agreed upon previously, overwhelmed these sounds.

23. NEW FAME

JIMMY RAEBURN SAUNTERED DOWN TOWN. HE WAS wearing his best clothes, because the other outfit had been ruined the day before. Yet, strange to say, his father had merely laughed at the destruction of valuable clothes. In fact, Jimmy was beginning to suspect that his father possessed a certain largeness of soul that had remained unsuspected all of these years. That morning he had said, "Jim, if you're going down town, you may want some money. So take a dollar along with you."

Whereupon, the first dollar of Jim's life was placed in his hand—a great, round, shining silver cartwheel of a dollar.

So Jimmy went down town. He left his house feeling distinctly conscious of the whiteness of the bandage that crossed his brown face. He had not gone half a block when Skinny hailed him from across the street. "Where goin', Jimmy?"

"Aw, just down the line," said Jimmy.

Skinny came along. In the next block Freckles Murphy joined—and Buddy Wainwright and Slim Jome and Doc Willis. Others fell in. It was a conclave that walked down the street with him, and people who saw the group pass trembled for the safety of windows and the welfare of chickens and pet cats.

As they came by Pudge Oliver's saloon they saw Pudge himself standing in front of the folding doors. His smile shone at Jimmy.

"Hello, Jim," said he. "Bringing the boys in for a drink?"

"Got any right good ginger ale?" asked Jimmy Raeburn.

"I've got the land's best!" said Pudge Oliver. "Come on in, boys."

They hesitated, awed and at the same time delighted. It was a forbidden place—forbidden to them by law and by their parents, to say nothing of that strange monster, public opinion. But in they went, and stood in the cool and fragrant shadows of that famous place where so many fighting men had stood—and fallen—under fire. Blue Barry Litton, among the others, had introduced himself to Holy Creek in this big room.

Pudge Oliver, apparently, knew all men by heart. He looked through them as though their hearts were overlaid by plate glass. Now Jimmy's crowd stood ranged down that celebrated bar and rested their proud feet upon the brass railing. They reached up high to put their elbows on the edge of the bar, and down the length of that bar went spinning the little frosty bottles of ginger ale, and each rattled and danced to a halt in its rightful position, ready to be poured. They shouted in gay applause for that. Then they poured out the drinks and stood with glasses poised.

They drank. The sting mounted through the nose to the eyes. They gasped and strangled with delicious pain. They laughed at one another and drank again. The world was a jolly world; this was a famous moment in their lives!

The ginger ale finished, Jimmy Raeburn pushed across the bar that huge silver dollar.

"Take it out of this, Pudge," said he.

"Thanks," said Pudge, and made change with a wonderful speed. The cash register had hardly stopped clanking and ringing when he dropped a pile of small change before the boy; and Jimmy, carelessly picked it up, dropping it into his pocket.

They filed out to the street, waving their hands at Pudge Oliver; and he, with a grave nod and a wave of the hand, followed them with his bright little eyes that held a shadow in them more profound, perhaps, than ever had been there before.

In the street, Jimmy casually glanced over the cash that remained to him. It was indeed a heap of silver. It contained, in fact, a whole dollar—not a penny had been subtracted from his new fortune.

"Wait a minute!" he called to the boys, and dashed back into the saloon. "Hey, Pudge," said he, panting, "you made a mistake. You gave me back a whole dollar."

"Hold on," said Pudge, staring with real alarm. "You mean to say I handed you back a whole dollar?"

Jimmy laughed, with a gasp in the laughter. Honesty was all right, of course, but it hurt.

"Yeah," he said, "there's the whole dollar. You take out your part." He dropped the money on the counter. A dime hit the floor, and when he had pursued and caught it—nothing can roll and dodge like a ten cent piece!—he straightened to find Pudge Oliver staring before him like one who sees far off unhappiness.

"I'm getting old, Jim," Pudge told the boy. "It's a sure sign when a fellow begins to make the wrong change. You know how I keep myself in mind of making the right change?"

"How?" said the boy.

"Well," said Pudge Oliver, "when I make a mistake in change, I never take the money back. There's not many that come back and offer it, matter of fact. But them that do—I just give the money back to 'em. Lost as much as a dollar and six bits that way, son. But it pays me in the end! It makes me say, 'Pudge, you got to be careful!"

He pushed the little stack of silver back across the bar.

"You go and take this, Jimmy," said he. "It ain't much, and it'll help me to remember."

It seemed a strange rule to Jimmy, but then—grown men are so often strange!

He took the money. "Seems kind of funny, Pudge," he said. "I don't like to get something for nothing."

"You get the drink, and I get the lesson," said Pudge. "We break even."

Jimmy's troupe went up the street.

"Is that him, Bob?" said one of a pair of cowpunchers who leaned against the wall of the tobacco shop. They were strangers to Jimmy.

"Yeah, that's young Raeburn," said the second of the pair.

Jimmy flushed a little and looked straight ahead, ignoring this delightful fame.

A sudden roar came from up the street. It was a shouting mob, yelling, dancing, singing, whooping; and as they went, Jimmy saw above their shoulders the strange picture of two black men, covered with dust and feathers, and grasping the thin edge of the rails on which they were being carried along.

"Tar and feathers!" yelled one of Jimmy's companions. "Those are the two that come to get Blue Barry—I just heard something about it a while ago. *Look* at 'em!"

Jimmy's companions dispersed, but one of the two men at the tobacco store called to Jimmy, "Hello!—Wait a minute!"

Jimmy paused. "Hello," he said. " 'S matter?"

"Got something to put up to you, Jim. You remember me, I guess?"

"Sure," said Jimmy, politely, vainly raking the leaves of his usually accurate memory. "Sure I remember you." He approached closer.

A confidential hand was laid on his shoulder.

"It's this way, Jim," said the cowboy. "Some of us boys wanta arrange a surprise for Blue Barry. Understand?"

"Sure," said Jimmy.

Said the other cowboy, "You know Litton better'n

anybody else does. You'd know what his taste is, wouldn't you?"

Jimmy flushed, dizzy with joy and pride. Grown men consulting him! It was better than being rich on a deathless dollar.

"Well," said Jimmy, "I know Barry pretty well, but I ain't sure I could guess what he'd want. I couldn't do that. He's pretty rich, you see."

"Sure he is.—It ain't the price of the thing that counts, though. It's the idea of it—to show him that we think a lot of him."

It was a phrase that Jimmy had heard many times. "I'll try to think of something," he said.

"Come along now, Jim," said the other. "We'll go off somewhere and talk it all over." And he hooked his arm through that of the boy. The cowboy called Bob stepped over to the other side and slipped his hand through Jimmy's other arm. They seemed a companionable pair, these two strange cowboys.

24. COMMITTEE-CHAIRMAN

THE FELLOW CALLED BOB, AS HE WALKED ALONG WITH Jimmy, swayed to the right as he went, as though his right leg did not give him absolutely certain support.

"We all decided that we oughta ask you," he said. "That's why you were named on the committee—the first thing. That's why they went and made you the chairman of the committee, to see about getting a surprise for Blue Barry."

"What does a chairman do?" asked Jimmy.

"The chairman's the head man, sort of the president or something," said the other cowboy, and as he said it, Jimmy, looking at him, noticed that he had a scarred chin. "They elected you the chairman, all of the boys did."

The boy was dizzy with pride. "Well, if they made me the chairman, I'd oughta accept, I guess.—But what's the good of going clean away from Holy Creek, like this?" he added.

"We wanta get away, where nobody'll overhear us," said the man with the scarred chin. "We got some hosses over here that might be a good surprise for him."

"Have you?" said Jimmy. "But he's got the mare, you know. I dunno that you could get another horse like her!"

"No, you couldn't, maybe," said the cowboy who limped. "But we got some horses that would make a bang-up second for her. And Barry Litton, he's a fellow that rides a lot, and he oughta have two beauties in his string."

"Well," said Jimmy, "I've heard him say that a gun, a woman, and a horse has gotta be picked by the man that's going to use 'em."

"There you go!" said Bob, admiringly. "Just what I said at the meeting—you know Barry like a book!"

"Oh, I don't know him like a book," said Jimmy. "He'd be too long for me to read—and the *words* would be too long, too."

He laughed a little as he said it, and the other two joined in heartily. The cowboys seemed full of the best of feeling and fellowship. By this time, they were well behind the town, and travelling towards a little grove of trees. It was there, they said, that the horses were waiting.

A little sting of suspicion touched Jimmy, unaccountably enough. "Why would you wanta hide out the horses like that?" he asked, coming to an abrupt halt. He looked up at his new companions.

The man with the scar on his chin suddenly set his jaw and pressed his lips together. For an instant he seemed to measure the distance to the trees. Then Bob, as he limped along, spoke up.

"Why, bless your heart, Jimmy!—What you think?" he said with a short, disarming laugh. "Would we walk right into town with the horses, and ask people which one they thought would do for Blue Barry?"

"No," said Jimmy, nodding. "No, I guess you wouldn't wanta do that!"

"Sure we wouldn't," said Scarface.

They reached the grove, and in the dark, cool center of it they came upon three tethered, saddled horses. Jimmy cried out when he saw them, for they had fine, hot-blooded lines, and their bony heads spoke of nothing but brains and breeding.

Jimmy fingered the softly working shoulder muscles of a bay, the central horse of the trio.

"Yeah, that's a horse, brother!" said Bob. *"That's* a horse that maybe could run down Barry's mare—no matter what she is!"

"Run her down?" exclaimed Jimmy, shrill with defiance. "Say, she's like wind blowing, that's all she's like!"

Bob said, "Suppose you get up and try the bay, eh?"

"Well, yeah, I might do that," said the boy, climbing into the saddle, sitting rather ill-at-ease on the lofty horse, which began to dance under him.

The man on his right mounted in turn, and so did Bob, who kept the lead rope of the bay.

"I'll take the rope," said Jimmy.

"It's safer this way," said Bob, with a quick glance at his companion.

And off they started at a gently swinging canter.

The bay gelding moved like a silken string, and handled like a hunting dog.

Presently, Jimmy shouted, "Why, Barry will go crazy when he gets onto this!"

"Will he?" answered Bob, pleasantly. "Now try him. down this slope, here.—Let him out for a mile, brother, and see some travelling that *is* travelling!"

Jimmy let the bay go. It was like letting go of a stone—and being pulled after it. For the bay's pace seemed to accelerate, even to the very end of that glorious mile of sprinting. The horse ran so fast that the man with the scar on his chin was dropped lengths and lengths behind and Bob's horse was an anchor dragging at the end of the tethering rope.

"Pull up!—Pull up!" yelled Bob.

The boy obeyed, laughing and gasping for breath, for there is something in the excitement of a hard gallop that takes the wind.

"He's a grand horse!" he shouted, forgetful that the wind of the gallop had died down and that shouting was unnecessary.

The bay turned his fine head a little, as though listening,

129

and lifted his head, also, as though proud of what he heard.

"He's a beautiful horse!" repeated Jimmy. "This is the thing to give Barry.—I suppose we'd better turn back?"

Bob twisted about in his saddle and glanced back. The town was lost far behind the hill which that beautiful mile of sprinting had raised to the rear.

Then he faced Jimmy with a hard face.

"We're not going back, brother.—We're going on," said he.

The shock of that made the boy grab the horn of the saddle with both hands. Then, realizing what this meant, he tried to jerk the bay around and flee. A reaching fist knocked him senseless from the saddle.

Jimmy wakened to find that he was hung over the withers of a horse. Twisting a little, he looked up into the face of Bob. It had been a pleasant face before. It was a grim one now.

"I told you he'd get over it," said Bob to his companion. "Gimme a hand, Jay, and we'll get him back into his saddle."

They halted, and Jimmy was quickly shifted back into place on the bay gelding.

He rode a while with his eyes closed, his head ringing, red sparks flying before his eyes. He was half nauseated, also; but as that sensation diminished, a worse one took its place. It was fear.

"How'd you get away the other night in the water, kid?" asked Bob.

"There was a bit of branch, sticking up over the surface of the pond," said Jimmy. "I got to that and kept just my face out of water. That way, I got my breath back. I climbed out when they went away."

"Humph!" said the other cowboy, adding, "You got into the Si Turner shack, later on. How'd you manage that?"

"I got on my mustang in the shed, and stuck along the side of it," said Jimmy. "That was all. You fellows happened to be on the other side of the horse, so you didn't see me hanging on. I steered it up to the window of the house, and then slid off inside the house and told Barry there was trouble coming. That's all."

"It's enough!" commented his questioner. "You hear that, Bob?"

"Yeah, I heard plenty of it," answered Bob. "Nervy brat, is what he is."

"What about Bill, the feller who got shot?" asked the man with the scar. He didn't seem really interested; merely curious.

"Barry's taking care of him. He won't die. Barry knows how to take care of a fellow."

"Barry'll see that he passes out," insisted Bob.

The boy was silent. Gloomily he stared down at the ground that flowed beneath him under the easy dog-trot of the bay gelding.

"Right now, I'm gonna tell you something," said Bob. "A lot of kids take long chances agin grown-ups. They figger that nobody'll be too hard with 'em. But lemme tell you that we got our orders to bear down—and down we're gonna bear! You don't mean nothing to us—you're just bait to catch Barry Litton. So if you get flip—if you try to get away—you're gonna catch a coupla slugs of lead where they won't do your digestion no good. Understand?"

Jimmy said nothing. There was no point in answering such a remark.

They entered a gap between hills, a place studded with great rocks, and pricked over with slender little pine trees. The fragrance of them hung in the air.

"It oughta be about here," said Bob's companion suddenly.

"Yeah, and here it is!" said Bob.

For a black horse stepped panther-like, silently, from behind a great bowlder, and on the horse sat a small and slender man with a thin face. He was rather handsome, and to Jimmy Raeburn his face was easily recalled to memory. It was the face of Rann Duval.

25. A MAN WHO'LL TALK

THE ONLY THOROUGHLY GOOD MERCHANDISE IN HOLY Creek, outside of guns in the Raeburn store, was to be found in the boot department of Hills and Mason's General Merchandise Store. Barry Litton appeared there late in the afternoon. Since the fire had burned them out, he needed apparel of many kinds, for himself and for Tom Willow. He slipped around and came in the back way, for whenever he appeared in the main street, people were instantly attracted to him and crowded about him. Feeling could not have been higher in his favor. He had done many spectacular things in Holy Creek, and this day the town as a whole had been able to make a gesture that showed something of its appreciation. Men are always more pleased when they have a chance to give, after much taking; and to a man Holy Creek was ready to stand with Barry Litton against the world! It wanted to tell him so to his face, and noisily. That was the reason Barry used the back entrance of the store.

Harry Mason himself was in the shop, and took him to the corner where the boots were kept. And as he fitted him, he said, "What's the matter, Barry?—Don't you like the front door?"

"I hear some of the boys are looking for me," said Litton, "so I keep off the main street, if I can. I'm afraid."

Harry Mason laughed. "Say, Barry," said he. "You ever really afraid of anybody in your life?"

"Plenty of times," said Barry Litton. He looked narrowly before him, with a shake of his head. He almost wished that he had courage enough to explain how the fear of little Rann Duval haunted him now, night and day; but he could not bring himself to speak of the man.

Mason looked up with a grin, which vanished, as he saw the other's seriousness. "Well," he muttered, "we all have our little troubles."

132

He half forgot this moment of gloom when, the next instant, he found a boot into which Barry Litton's foot slipped with perfect ease.

Barry stood up, and as Lou Raeburn came into the store in haste, paid for the purchase.

"Hello, Barry," said she. "Where's Jimmy?"

"Jim? Haven't had a glimpse of him all day," he answered.

"Do you mean that?" she asked, her face growing very sober.

"Not a glimpse," said he. "Where is he?"

"I don't know," she answered. "He wasn't home for lunch. I thought——"

Barry shrugged his shoulders. "I'll find out where he is in ten minutes. He has a lot of friends who want to entertain him, to-day. Lou, do you know exactly what he did, last night?"

"He won't talk much about it," said the girl. "But of course everybody knows, in a general way."

"He's the gamest lad in the world!" said Litton. "There's another thing I'd like to speak about to you. Will you come out the side door for a minute?"

She went with him through the side door that opened upon a narrow little alley, between the wall of the building and the high board fence that surrounded it. As he looked down at her, a breeze touched them and set her dress to fluttering. He saw that she was trembling slightly, but the eyes she lifted were bluer than the eyes of Blue Barry, and just as steady.

"I'm going to ask a question," said Litton. "If you don't want to answer it—let it go."

"Fire away," said she.

"You know," said Litton, "the other night when you came to ask about Jimmy—was there something behind your coming? Something behind it that was not Jim?"

Manifestly, the question was a shock to her. He saw her swallow. He saw her make a strong effort, her eyes widening.

"You'll think I'm a fool," said she, "but I'll tell you. Jim came running home in an agony. He begged me to do something for him, and when I said that I would, he asked me simply to go to your house, and ask if he were there."

He exclaimed softly, with surprise. "I don't understand it!" he said.

"There was one other thing," she said. "He told me that I was to ask for him—and then put in something about the trust that my father and I feel for you—as a friend for Jimmy, you see?" She flushed hotly. "It isn't easy to say," she added, "but I've said it."

He looked away from her for a moment, muttering, "What did he know? That's the question!"

Then straight to Lou Raeburn, "I can't explain everything just now. But I'll tell you this. If you hadn't come, by this time, Tom Willow and I would have been running for our lives—on a train—hundreds of miles away from here! My nerve was gone—I was beaten. And if I'd run, I never would have been able to lift my head again. You kept me from that!"

"Will you tell me *how?*" she asked him, bewildered. "Jimmy was mysterious. You're even more so."

"I'll tell you why," he said. "You Raeburns, father and daughter and son, are the cleanest lot I've ever met in my life. And when I found out that you had put some decent trust in me, I couldn't run like a rat. Between the two of you—Jim and you—you could make the right kind of a man out of any tramp.—I'm going to look Jimmy up now.—I'm in a tangle, Lou, that's even deeper than the Dead Man Steer. If I get out of it, I'm coming straight back to you and ask for a permanent position in the Raeburn house—running errands, doing odd jobs, or anything I can get."

He left her suddenly. She leaned a hand against the door, and looked fixedly after him; but he turned the corner without glancing back.

Barry Litton walked on for half a block, his heart still beating fast after that encounter, a wild joy in his eye, and his step quick and light. Then he saw a tow-headed youngster, the darkness of whose skin almost obscured his freckles. He hailed him, and the boy sprang to attention with a jump.

"Yeah, Barry?" he asked. For there wasn't a boy in that town who did not yearn with his inmost heart to pass to fame in the companionship of Barry Litton, as Jimmy Raeburn had done.

"Where's Jim? Seen him?" asked Litton.

"Not since the tar and featherin'," said the other. "Me and some more that are real friends of his, we went down town with him, and he gave us a drink at Pudge Oliver's—"

"Drink?" said the big man.

"Ginger ale," grinned the boy. "Afterwards, we got another treat from Jimmy. He was *full* of money. And then come the crowd with Craven and Jones.—*They* won't be man-catchin' for a while, Barry—nor anybody else that comes to this town for you, I guess! But in the crowd, I lost all sight of Jim."

"You did? Where'd you see him last?"

"Down by the corner of the tobacco store—"

Barry went to the tobacco store. A one-legged, yellow-faced man kept that store; he was beloved by the entire town, because it was he who had organized the town baseball team, and often paid its travelling expenses, or the expenses of teams from neighboring villages who came to play. It was his one virtue, but it was enough.

"See Jimmy?" asked Barry Litton.

"Didn't see him, Litton," said the tobacco man. "Not since this morning, when he was talkin' to a coupla gents just outside the shop, here.—I got some news, Barry. I got a letter from the fastest doggone shortstop that ever ate up the hot ones, and he's gonna come here to town and look for a job. If we can find a place for him we'll . . ."

"Good news!" said Litton. "But who were the fellows Jim was talking to?"

"Never saw 'em before," said the other, "but—"

"Never saw 'em before? Are you sure? You know everybody in the town, I guess. You sure you never saw 'em before?"

"No, they were strangers, all right. Why, what's the matter, Barry?"

"What did they do?" asked Barry Litton, with a cold sinking of his heart.

"Why, they strolled off with Jimmy, after a while," said the other. "Jimmy's fit company for any of the cowpunchers, since you went and made him famous, Litton! And—"

"He hasn't been home all day; I haven't seen him all day; the boys in town haven't seen him.—He walked off

135

with two strangers." So Barry Litton summed up the matter, rapidly.

Then, without a word, he turned on his heel and strode out of the shop.

The tobacconist followed him to the door and blinked down the street after him. "Something's up agin," he said to himself. "It ain't a small thing that stirs up Litton. By jingo, he's runnin'!—There he stops a kid—there he runs agin. Sprintin', too—and yet it's a hot day."

It was a red-faced and panting Barry Litton that rode across the fields on the mare, finally, and reined up his horse at the verge of the swimming pool. Nine-tenths of the boys of Holy Creek were there, sitting in shadow or sun, some on the rocks, some on branches, some diverting themselves by shooting down a mud slide and splashing into the water.

They put up a yell when they saw him. "Hey, hello, Barry!" For a man who is the friend of one boy is, thereby, the friend of all the other boys in the world.

"Where's Jimmy?" he asked.

No one answered.

Barry stood in his stirrups. "If any one of you has seen Jimmy since this morning, when he was outside the tobacco shop—speak out!"

There was not a murmur—not a whisper of sound. And as the sense of disaster struck home in Barry, like a bullet, he thought of blue-eyed Lou Raeburn, as he had last seen her, and pulled the mare around with a groan.

Almost instantly, he was back at the old Si Turner place. The dying embers of the burned shack were still putting up a few wisps of smoke, here and there, above their coverings of ashes.

Litton leaped from the mare into the horse shed.

The doctor was still there with the wounded man, and he turned a happy face to Barry. "He's getting on," said the doctor, with a finger raised, cautioning silence. "Been sleeping for hours, now. No temperature. Pulse getting stronger right along. I cut out the two slugs that were in him. Both of 'em had gone almost through. It was an easy job. He's relaxed and easy. And—"

"He can stand waking up, then, for a minute?" said Barry Litton.

Tom Willow stood by, his arms folded.

"Saddle your mule, Tom," said the master. "We're going on a hard trail."

"With the Dead Man Steer?" asked the sailor.

"No, by ourselves. Nobody will bother about the steer, now, I think—not for a day or two, perhaps. Here's a pair of boots that ought to fit you."

Barry left Willow, and went on to where the sleeping man lay. He sat down beside him, and instantly the man's eyes opened. He smiled faintly at Litton.

"How's things, partner?" he asked.

"I told you I wouldn't ask questions," said Barry Litton, "but I have to now. They've grabbed Jimmy Raeburn and run off with him."

"You mean the youngster?—The freckle-faced kid?— Your friend, Barry?"

"Yes. Will you talk?"

The other closed his eyes for a moment, and grew pale. Then he looked straight back at Litton.

"I'll tell you everything I know!" he said.

26. A CALL ON THE JUDGE

LITTON NODDED. "I KNOW WHAT IT MEANS TO YOU TO talk," said he. "But they'll never know from me that you said a word. What sort of an assignment were you on, all you fellows who came here with Duval?"

"To get you," said the wounded man. "Nothing else counted. The boy and Willow were on your side of the fence. Duval says to us that the kid is small, but that he's got a real pair of eyes and ears. We're to try to block him out—and a bullet for Willow if we get a chance. The Dead Man Steer—that comes last in the picture. You're what he wants to get, and he wants you bad!"

"Then you think that if they've got Jimmy they may— er—?" He paused.

"Bump him off?—Not if he doesn't make trouble, or unless they find him in the way. But there's gents in that outfit, Barry, that would murder a boy or a woman as easy as nothing at all, if Duval said the word."

Litton drew out a handkerchief and mopped his forehead. The world seemed a huge place, and Jimmy Raeburn a very small particle to find in the great sea of space.

"Where d'you think I might find headquarters?" he asked.

"I don't know. We shifted every day. That's Duval's game—always on the move."

"You wouldn't know where to go to find him now, if you were able to ride a horse?"

"No more idea than the man in the moon!"

"He's not working for nothing. Do you know where he gets the money? The Chaneys or the Morgans, or both of 'em?"

"I only know this: I rode to the Chaney house with a message for the Judge. I know that Blister Matthews went to the same place with another message."

"How did the Judge treat you?"

"Like a jewel that he wanted to keep in the dark," grinned the other. "He talked mighty soft and mighty few, and gave me an envelope to carry back. It had a soft feel—like greenbacks."

"Then Chaney's the man," said Litton. "Well, take things easy, partner. After this, I'm your friend. So long!"

"Are you taking that trail?" asked the wounded man.

"I'm taking it."

"God help you, then!" said Bill. "Here's wishing you luck!" He gave Barry's hand a faint grip, and then closed his eyes with a weary shake of the head.

In a few seconds Barry was in the saddle, and Tom Willow was on the mule beside him. From the corral came a heavy bellowing, and Litton looked across at the Dead Man Steer, which stood in the center of the area, lowing with a note as mournful as that of a wolf.

"Dead Man is the name—and dead men it's gonna be now, eh?" asked Tom Willow, studying his chief's face with care and awe.

"They've stolen Jimmy Raeburn," said Litton. "Come on. Make that mule trot."

Steadily they drilled through the yellow of the late after-

138

noon; and then among the bleak, sandy hills they rode through the dusk, and into the deep, black heart of the night. Gradually the stars came down from the upper sky and burned close. The cool of the night wind began to touch them like a mercy. And all of the way Barry Litton had not spoken a word to his companion.

Now he paused in a growth of high shrubbery. "You see those lights in the hollow—through the trees, Tom?" he asked.

"Yes, I see 'em."

"Take the mare and keep her for me. Loosen the cinches and let her have a breath. After fifteen minutes, cinch her up again. We may be travelling once more, about that time."

"Where, sir?" asked Tom Willow.

"I don't know. To hell, maybe."

"We been bound there for a long time," muttered Willow, and stared after his chief as the latter strode down the hollow and was quickly lost to view.

The house was unremarkable except for the trees that grew around it, which the Judge's care had nourished until they were tall and strong. The house itself was merely a long super-shack, with a veranda strung out along its entire face. The family quarters were at one end of the veranda, and toward the other end was the bunk house, where the cowpunchers lived.

As Barry Litton came through the last screen of foliage in front of the house, he saw what he had expected, the whole Chaney family sitting on the veranda in the darkness and cool of the night. From the double front door a stream of light poured out and showed to the watcher two young men, an elderly woman and a girl, all chatting together. The Judge was walking up and down behind the others, his hands clasped behind his back. His words, whenever he spoke, were obscured by the cigar which he was smoking.

It was a peaceful scene. In the bunk house some one was crooning a song, playing a banjo accompaniment. The heat of the day was still seeping up from the ground, but the wide night received it, and poured down coolness in exchange. For all of that seeming peace, however, it was clear that the Judge's mind was troubled, if the irregularity of his pacing steps was any indication.

Litton circled behind the trees, and came out in front of the bunk house. He mounted the steps, then turned; and teetering back and forth, from heel to toe, with folded arms, he seemed to be admiring the coolness of the night.

"Hello, there!" called the Judge's voice.

"Hello!" said Litton.

"You boys are supposed to keep off the veranda this time of night," said the Judge curtly.

"Wanted to see you a minute, Judge," said Litton.

"Not my office hours, and you know it," said the Judge. "Save it for the morning." He turned away.

"It's the kind of thing that would spoil before the morning," said Litton.

The Judge whirled about. "What's that you say?" he called out.

"It's pressing," said Litton.

"Young man," said the Judge, "who are you? I've spoken twice, and you're still on the veranda.—Come here to me!"

Litton approached with a slow and diffident step. "Why, Judge," he said, "what I wanted to tell you about is a thing that you'll want to know, I think."

The Judge's temper went with a snap that was almost audible. He took several rapid steps towards Litton, saying, "I don't need anybody to do my thinking for me! Who are you to—?"

They were close now.

"I'm Barry Litton, and here's my card," said Litton, dropping the muzzle of a revolver against Judge Chaney's stomach.

The latter said nothing, but his whole body wavered as though he had been struck.

"You fat, sneaking, poisonous rat," said Blue Barry softly, "don't move. They've taken Jimmy Raeburn.—Where have they put him?"

"Father," called the girl, "Buck wants to know if—" She came running as she spoke.

"Stop her!" said Litton softly.

"Go back, Mary," said the Judge. "I'm talking business."

She stopped. "But I only wanted to know—" she began.

140

Her father roared, "Go back and leave me alone! Can't I have any peace in my own home?"

Slowly she turned away.

Said Litton, "Where's Jimmy Raeburn? Quick, Judge! I'm behind schedule already."

"I don't know," muttered the Judge. "I don't understand anything that you say, Litton. Between you and me there's been a good deal of misunderstanding, and—"

"Between you and Rann Duval there's been a lot of coöperation, though, and that's what makes the difference."

"Rann—" gasped the Judge. Even in the darkness the visitor could see the other's lips struggling to form words that would not come.

"You hired Duval," said Litton. "You brought him here to put me out of the way, and to get back the Dead Man Steer for you.—And his heart's in the job, I'll say that!

"I've got you in the palm of my hand, Judge. I only need to close the fingers, and they'll hang you, you murdering crook. But that wouldn't save Jimmy. Those devils of yours would brain him and throw him in a hole, or leave him for the wolves to eat.—Where am I to find Rann Duval? Come, out with it!"

"Litton," said the Judge, "it's a shocking thing that you're saying to me. No matter how I feel about your outrageous conduct to me, young man, the fact remains that little children never have anything to fear from me. My hand, I thank God, has protected the young and helped the innocent, and—"

"By Heaven," said Litton, "it would be such a splendid service to the world if I sank a chunk of lead through the middle of your heart that I'm more than half tempted to do it!—Are you going to answer me? Where's Rann Duval?"

"Has Jimmy Raeburn disappeared?" muttered the Judge.

"He has. Where's Duval? This is the last time I'll ask you. I'll open you up and see what's written inside next!—You're taking a stroll with me, Judge, down into the trees," he added.

"Wait a minute!" gasped the Judge. "I'll talk, man!—About the boy, I never dreamed—I never knew—my

141

whole influence would have been against— But Rann Duval is in Cedar Crossing—across the hills, near that town. You know the place?"

"I've heard about it."

"Back in the hills there's a 'dobe shack."

"Yes?"

"You'll spot it easily. One tree stands beside it—one scraggly old cedar that seems about to fall. The shack is in a hollow between the hills. Where's your horse now?"

"Back behind the house, and up the draw," lied Blue Barry.

"Turn to your right out of the draw, and head for the sugarloaf. You'll see it against the stars, even now. Go straight for that, and it'll take you to the hut. That's Duval's headquarters."

"How long will he be there?"

"Two or three days, I suppose."

"All right, Judge. Now just walk with me down into the trees, will you?"

"My God, boy!" whispered the Judge. "D'you mean murder?"

"I ought to kill you, true.—That wouldn't be murder," said Blue Barry. "But I've implied a bargain with you, and I'll keep my side of it. You can trust my word, Judge. You've been a crook in other things, but you've been straight as a ruled line in your cattle business. I've been a crook, too; but I keep my word when I give it. You walk down into the trees with me, though. It'll give me a chance to get a head start, before you've handed on the alarm to your cowpunchers."

The Judge drew in a quick, deep breath. It came out again with a hissing sound.

"I'll go," he said. "There's honor to be found—" He did not say, "with thieves." Checking himself, he called over his shoulder, "I'm strolling down into the trees for a minute. Be back soon."

They went from the veranda and into the lofty, dark night that was gathered in the woods. And the Judge, though the night was growing cooler, panted heavily as he walked.

"About the boy," he said. "I give you my word, Litton—I know nothing. I know nothing at all. If the suspicion that you have is correct—then the shock of such a thing—"

By this time they were well into the screen of deeper darkness.

"Judge, I'll leave you here," Litton interrupted. "I'm going on a trail where, I suppose, I'll leave my hair behind me. Anyway, think things over. Murder's not so sweet—no matter how small a price you have to pay the murderer. So long!" He stepped quickly behind a tree trunk, then hurried off through the pitchy blackness.

27. A GAGGED MAN

BARRY MOVED AWAY FROM JUDGE CHANEY IN A LINE parallel with the front of the house, as though intending to circle around it; but the moment he was well on his way he angled off that line and sprinted at full speed back to the spot where he had left Tom Willow.

The latter was in the saddle as his chief came up. "Are they on the way?" demanded Tom in a shaken voice.

"Get out of the saddle!" said Barry. "We haven't much time. I've been swapping lies with the Judge. His lies were a little bigger than mine, but I think that I may be able to do a little better guessing than he can do, in the windup."

Willow stood beside him. "You gotta remember, chief," said he, "that when a rub comes and there's any galloping, this here mule ain't as fast as a horse."

"I'll remember you, Tom, when the pinch comes," said Barry Litton. "I'm going to keep you with me to-night, not really for the rub, but as a reserve after the rub comes.—Don't worry. But you have the best eyes in the world for seeing at night.—Keep your eyes moving. Try to spot anything that comes out of that wood, in front of the house. In two minutes there ought to be a rider, and unless I've missed that guess, he'll come this way."

143

The horses were pressed back to a spot where the tall brush quite enshrouded them. Then the two took up their places on the brow of the hill, and strained their eyes toward the woods, behind which glimmered the lights from the House of Chaney.

It was Tom Willow who first exclaimed, "There—over to the right. There's a rider coming, chief."

"We'll have to chase him, then," muttered Litton. "I'd hoped that he'd string out and come this way! It's the natural trail out from the Chaney house—travelling in this direction."

"He *is* coming this way!" exclaimed the sailor. "Aye, and he's burning up the ground. Look at him, will you? Like a bird, he's sailin' over the earth."

Out of the dimness of the hollow the rider rose, grew clearer, and stood up gigantic against the starry sky.

Litton rose from the brush with a ready Colt. "Hold up, brother!" he called.

A curse was jolted out of the rider as his mustang halted on planted, sliding feet, before the reins had been so much as touched. The suddenness of the stop flung the rider forward on the pommel. As he straightened, Litton's revolver was under his breast.

"Steady, old son!" said Litton. "Never mind your gun. Just reach."

"Who are you?" demanded the rider as he obeyed.

"I'm Litton."

"That skunk of a Chaney told me you'd be the other way from the house."

"Lying is his one best hold," agreed Litton.

"The bronk beat me more than you did," declared the puncher. "The fool stopped before I had a chance to make my play."

"You had the bad luck," answered Litton. "Now just slide out of the saddle."

The cowboy threw his leg over the horn of the saddle and slid to the ground.

"Tie him up," said Litton to Tom Willow.

That order was not needed. Tom would as soon have been naked as without plenty of strong twine; and instantly his active hands and his sailor knots were securing the hands of the other behind his back.

In the meantime, Litton talked.

"Who are you, partner?" he asked.

"That makes no difference," growled the captive.

"It makes a difference to me," answered Litton. "We'll start with names. I'm Barry Litton."

"Litton," said the other, "is it a fact that you walked in on the Judge and picked him right off his own veranda?"

"There was nothing else to do," said Litton. "I had to have a chat with him.—Your name, old son?"

"Chuck Whalen, if you gotta know."

"I've heard of you, Chuck. I've heard of you and your two guns. You simply had a bad break to-night."

"I've had a break," said Chuck Whalen, "that'll ruin me.—I'll have to leave the range, after this here!"

"Chuck, will you talk turkey with me?"

"Sure I will. What else can I do?"

"What did the Judge say to you, or give you? And where did he send you?"

"He came out of the woods and back to the house with a yell," said Whalen. "He hollered to one of the boys to saddle up the best hoss in the stable. He hollered to me to ride that hoss as fast as I could—make it hump, and get to Tom Chaney's house in time to tell him that you were loose and on the warpath. He said young Jimmy Raeburn had disappeared, and that Rann Duval was suspected of workin' on the Chaney side."

"That's a long message," said Barry Litton.

"Yeah, it is."

"Now let's have the real one."

"That's the real one."

Litton stepped close. "Your crowd," he said, "has taken to bearing down on twelve-year-old youngsters. Do you think, Whalen, that I'll hesitate to tear what I want to know right out of your heart?—Why, no, brother. There's nothing in the world that I want but an excuse to get started. Understand?"

"Why, man, I'm talking true," said Chuck Whalen.

"We'll burn it out of him," said Litton to Tom. "Throw a noose around him—"

"Wait a minute," said Whalen. "I've held out. You gotta admit that."

"You told a lie—and a good lie," said Litton. "But it had to be wrong. Now let me have the facts!"

145

"I just ride like the devil across country to Duval, and tell him that you're on the loose. That's all."

"Are you sure?"

"Dead sure."

"Anything about the boy?"

"Not a word."

"Any letter?"

"No."

"I'll take a look for myself, if you don't mind."

"It's in the breast pocket of my shirt, then—and be damned to you!" said Whalen.

Litton found the envelope, opened it, and by the light of a match he read the contents.

It was a short note, but filled with meat. There was no address and no signature, and the letters were printed neatly but swiftly with pencil, not ink. They said:

Litton is on the trail after Jimmy Raeburn. Bad mistake to take the boy. The town will rise against me—and the Morgans, too. Try to do something about it. Either return him to town or dispose of him some place near Holy Creek, so that it will seem an accidental death.

"Accidental death!" murmured big Blue Barry. "I know the kinds of accidental death that Stacey has up his sleeve."

"Who's Stacey?" asked Whalen.

"An old friend of mine," said Litton. "Tom, tie his hands to his feet, and gag him."

"Are you gonna leave me here to strangle?" exclaimed Whalen. "I'd rather have it out of a gun, or from the end of a knife, Litton!"

"You'll take what you can get," answered Litton. "Fix him Tom, but fix it so he can breathe."

And Tom, as he worked, was muttering gloomily, "Look at the time we're wastin' over them! Here's a hound all mixed up in murder. Would any of them hesitate to slip a knife between our ribs? No! And proud and glad would be the gent that done it. But you and me, we tie 'em—so they can breathe, even—and then we don't so much as brand 'em.—And that's the devil, chief! A twist of the wrist, and Whalen, here, would be so far away he'd never find his way back to the world again. But you won't have it that way."

"I'm a deputy sheriff," said the other, "and I have to stay inside the law."

"That's a good one!" said Whalen. "That's rich enough to—"

His voice was obliterated, for as he spoke, the strong and ungentle hand of the sailor had jammed the gag between his teeth.

28. MIDNIGHT PARLEY

"WHAT'S THE MATTER, TOM?" ASKED BLUE BARRY.

"He kind of give me a pain, was all," said Tom Willow. "Him and the way he talked give it to me! If his hands was free, I'd like to take a punch at him."

"Steady—and take that gag away for a minute," commanded Barry Litton.

The thing was done, grudgingly.

"Is that the way you wanta choke a man?" the victim gasped. "Why not shoot him straight off, and be done with it?"

"I might leave you here without a gag," said Litton. "But I want directions to find Rann Duval. Got 'em handy?"

Said the prisoner, "It's like this, brother—you ride only about three miles from here.—I don't mind telling you. Duval'll murder me for it, but—"

"He won't know," said Litton.

"He always knows," said Whalen. "He knows everything that's done and said. It ain't safe to think even a thousand miles from Rann Duval."

"You know him, I see," murmured Litton.

"Yeah. I know him. But it's better to die by him than by a gag.—You ride three miles. You climb most of the way, and you get to a range of black hills—you can see 'em yonder, from here. I dunno why they look black, but they are. They got a lot of pine trees growin' on 'em."

"I've seen the hills," said Barry. "Where do we go in them?"

"There's a broad valley, with hummocks thrown up in it, like mole hills done big. In the middle of that there valley is a hill; and all I know, I tell you straight. I ride to the foot of that hill, and there's one rock sticking up that ain't blackish like the rocks around it. Instead, it's kind of red, veined around with white. I take and stop beside that rock and give a coupla hollers, like this, "Halloo! Halloo-oo-oo!" Then I climb down, and make a cigarette and smoke. Pretty soon, along comes somebody or other—"

"Duval?"

"No, never him. But along comes somebody, and wants to know what's what. I tell him; and if I got a letter, I give him that letter, and then I go back to the ranch. That's all I know, and you can cut my throat wide, but you ain't gonna be able to get anything more out of it! I've told you the truth."

"I knew that by the face of it," said Litton. "I'd like to turn you loose, Whalen, but I can't risk that. You can get back to the ranch by rolling, if you want to. We've got to start along."

"That ranch'll never see me agin," said Whalen, "if ever I get a fair shot to pull out of here. And lemme tell you, I mean it! Doggone me, but I feel sort of lonesome, when I see you boys mount.—So long, Litton. You've done me better than I deserved to be done."

The two others were in their saddles by this time, and straightway they made for the black hills which had been described to them, and whose summits, like low-rolling smoke, extended along the edge of the horizon.

They rode at a dog-trot, the mare fidgeting to get into a gallop.

Among the hills they came to the hollow valley at last, where the darkness seemed to be rising from the dingy ground.

They could see, clearly, the hill that rose like a pyramid in the center of the valley. And here Barry Litton drew rein.

"You're the supply ship, Tom," he said. "You stay

148

here. Pull over there among the rocks, where you'll be out of sight in case anybody with sharp eyes and a lot of questions comes blundering along this way."

"What d'you do?" asked Willow. "Go in there and try to bust your neck?"

"I cruise around and look for something to happen."

The sailor answered, "Dead men are gonna happen. I feel that much in my bones."

"That's cheerful," said Litton. "If I'm not back here inside of two or three hours, you head for town and get the sheriff. Tell him ten good men would be better than fifty pick-ups, for a job like this."

"Yeah," growled Tom. "Ten men as good as you. That's all the sheriff would need."

"So long, Tom."

"Good-by," said Tom Willow, and held out his hand.

Litton found it, grasped it silently, and rode down into the hollow.

Even by daylight, the valley must have been a dreary place. By night, it seemed to be filled with mournful ghosts, looming ahead and turning into trees and rocks only when the rider was close up.

Barry came close to the rise of the hill and circled it a little, to the left, until he came to the rock that had been described to him by Whalen. It rose pale in the darkness, like an iceberg at sea.

He dismounted, and the mare tossed up her head and snorted, as though she scented something like danger near them.

"You're right, old girl," said her rider. Then he called, "Halloo!"

His voice was hushed by the awe of the dreary place. He raised it higher, "Halloo! Halloo-oo-oo!"

Then he waited. It seemed to him that minutes went by, and that still the echo of his voice was being faintly repeated, though he knew that it was sounding in his mind only. Presently, immediately before him, he heard a quiet step, and saw the figure of a man walking toward him.

The fellow came up close, and stood there silently, for a moment. He was about Blue Barry's height, but of a narrower build, it seemed. He wore an old hat with a

149

brim that flopped down about his head. In that dimness it looked almost like a hood.

"Who are you?" he demanded.

"That's all right," said Litton. "And the same to you—doubled up."

"Hey, what kind of a play is this?" asked the stranger, alarmed.

"I'm here because I rode here," Barry replied. "I'm looking for somebody who's not quite your size."

"What size might he be?"

"He's small."

"There's a lot of small men in the world."

"He's got a quiet way of speaking, but you don't forget what he says."

The tall fellow grunted and nodded. "Yeah, maybe you know what you're talking about. Who you from?"

"I'm from a friend of the little chap I've told you about."

"You gotta break out a few names for me, brother," said the man of the slouch hat, suspiciously.

"Names don't buy anything in this game," answered Litton. "Suppose you lead off with your own moniker?"

"My name'll sleep without being rocked in a cradle," said the other.

"Well, is he around here?" asked Litton.

"Is who around here?"

"The little guy I told you about."

"How would I know?"

"You want to keep me standing here all night?" asked Litton.

"Look here, you dummy," said the other. "Did you get orders to play this kind of a game when you got up here?"

"I got orders to send the letter straight. That's all I know."

"Well, let's have the letter, and maybe I can find the man it's for—the little man you were talkin' about."

"Steady up!" murmured Litton. "I hand it to the first man that asks for it—is that the dodge?"

"What's wrong about that?"

"Why," exclaimed Litton, "far as I know, you may be one of the sheriff's gang.—You might be Litton himself, for all I know."

The other chuckled. "You ever see Litton?"

"Yes."

"Well, when I light this smoke, you take a look at me."

He scratched a match, but before he put the flame to the end of his cigarette, he held it high, and looked straight at Blue Barry's face. By the same glow, Litton saw an unshaven, dark-skinned fellow. There was a sheen to the skin about his eyes and over the bridge of his nose. He was not a pretty picture. At some time or other his long nose had been broken by a blow, so that it was now twisted far to the side. His brown, glittering eyes stared eagerly and suspiciously into Litton's eyes.

Finally, he touched the last flicker of the match to the end of his cigarette. His cheek sucked hollow as he drew; then the match dropped into a thin red streak that went out on the ground.

There was a moment of silence. The stranger spat out some grains of tobacco.

"You may be all right," said Barry Litton. "The devil of it is, how'm I to know whether you're straight or not?"

"Yeah, how can you tell, except you was sent here, and told to holler. Why didn't one of the other boys come up with the letter you talk about?"

"You mean Whalen?"

"You know Whalen, do you?"

"Yeah. Sure I know him. Why wouldn't I know Whalen, if I know anything?"

"That sounds like something," declared the man of the broken nose. "But far as I know, *you* might be Litton. Doggone me if you don't look a lot like him!"

"Do I?—I'm tired of hearing that. You poor cock-eyed owl, did you ever lay an eye on Barry Litton?"

"Yeah. Sure I've laid an eye on him, and he's a ringer for you!"

"I've heard *that* said, too," said Litton. "I don't take it for a compliment, if you ask me."

"He ain't good enough for you to be like him—is that it?"

"He's a big soggy hound," said Litton. "Some day I'm going to be all square with him."

"Has he got something on you?"

"He's got a little something. But if you think he looks like me, he's twenty pounds heavier."

151

"Yeah, he's bigger, all right. Now, what you wanta do about this? You got a letter. Gonna give it to me?"

"Not till you uncork something that shows you're right. I can't take chances. You're a fool if you expect me to."

"Wait a minute," said the other. "I'll think up something that'll show you—" His voice died out. Then he said, "The kid's planted."

"My God!" exclaimed Litton. "Have they—killed—Jimmy Raeburn?"

"Does that hurt you?"

"I'm fond of kids. He was a fresh brat, but he was all right," said Litton. He recovered himself, seeing that he had been close to dangerous ground, and though his heart ached at what he had heard, he managed to say, carelessly, "Well, what's a fool boy—one way or another—in the sort of game we're playing?"

"Well," said the man of the slouch hat, "the kid ain't really dead. When I said he was planted, I meant he's planted safe with us, here. If I know about him at all, that shows I'm on the inside, don't it?"

"I suppose it does."

"Then pass me over the letter, and tell me anything that's to be told."

"Why shouldn't I tell Duval himself?"

"He's not seeing anybody, to-night. He's sitting by himself, and thinking."

"What's the matter with him?—Sick?"

"Sort of sick, I guess. He hates to have a plan flivver."

"And he and his gang flivvered last night," agreed Litton.

"How would anybody think that a fool kid, twelve years old, would have the nerve and the brains that this here Jimmy Raeburn flashed on us last night?"

"He broke up the plans," agreed Litton. "I don't see why more men weren't used, though. There were a lot of us at the ranch that Duval could have used."

"Could he?" said the other. "Well, Duval likes his own pick—and the pick of nobody else."

"That's his business, but his game went flop," said Litton.

"And that's why he's sitting and having a think. The *next* play he makes won't go flop, though. You can put your money on that!"

"So I've got to pass on the message to you, have I?"

"It looks that way, brother."

"I may catch the devil for this," muttered Litton.

"Yeah," said the other indifferently. "You just gotta take your chances that I'm right, if you can't make up your mind by what I've told you."

"Well, here's the news," said Litton. "Holy Creek has missed Jimmy Raeburn, and everybody suspects that Rann Duval's gang has grabbed him. The people are pretty nearly crazy. You know what that means."

"I dunno that I'm bothered any what the people of Holy Creek are thinking," said the man of the slouch hat.

"Sure you're not," answered Litton. "But you'd be interested, *pronto,* if any of them got their hands on you, and found that you were with Duval.—They'd burn us all alive, boy, that's what they'd do. They'd burn us an inch at a time. Child-stealing isn't so popular around this neck of the woods." He held out his hand. "You can tell Duval that the Judge is in a terrible stew. He's walking around in circles, like a locoed bull. He gave me this letter, without so much as an envelope on it. That's how rattled he is."

"You know what's in the letter?"

Litton stepped closer, and tapped the other on the shoulder.

"Brother," he said, "even if I'd read it, I'd forget it in five seconds.—So would you, if you've got a brain. So long!"

"Going back?—Wait a minute! Duval may want to send an answer."

"Nothing was told me about waiting for answers," said Litton, stubbornly. "I've done my job, and I'm going back. So long!"

The other called him a fool, but Barry was already in the saddle, and had turned his mare's head.

29. OVERHEARD

BARRY DID NOT RIDE FAR, HOWEVER. HE SIMPLY turned the horse around the big, pale rock; and then, seeing that the fellow of the slouch hat had disappeared into the woods again, he hurried the mare back to the edge of the trees. There he forced her into a thick coppice, and with a word, made her lie down. Rifle bullets might strike her and kill her as she lay there, but they would never be able to sting her into rising and revealing herself to searchers.

Then, eager with haste but stealthy with fear of what might lie before him, Litton stole rapidly forward through the trees, feeling his way with his hands outstretched, and putting his feet down toes first, so that he might judge the ground he was walking on.

Even then, he would not have been able to overtake the man of the slouch hat, had it not been that presently he saw before him a flare of light among the trees. Stealing closer, he made out the pale square of a paper held close to a man's face.

The light went out; the letter had been read. Curiosity had overmastered that broken-nosed fellow; and now, as he went forward again, Barry Litton followed easily behind him, putting his feet down exactly when the other stepped, so that possible noises he made might seem to the other to have been made by his own steps.

Barry expected that his guide would go to a horse, mount it, and head away from the hill; then, when Barry had found the correct direction, he would follow with the mare, at full speed. But now he saw the light of a fire breaking through the tree trunks, and staining the ground before him with long splashes of yellow-red.

The light increased. He had glimpses of black, moving shadows that swept monstrously across the immobile darkness of the trees. He saw the flames themselves, sparkling.

Then he was close enough to hear the voices.

On the very edge of a little clearing he stopped, and saw a dozen men seated about a fire; and with his first glance, he picked out Jimmy Raeburn and Rann Duval. It was not hard to find them with the eyes, because they sat close together, but a little distance separating them from the others. They were like a king and a prince before a court—a court composed of chosen rascals. Barry, in his time, had known many a dark criminal; but these seemed the flower of the whole villainous race. The man of the broken nose was handsome, compared with many of them. It was not a matter of features; it was the sheer hideousness of motive and impulse that glared out of their eyes or was drawn in the sneering or sullen lines of their mouths.

He of the slouch hat went towards his chief, and little Rann Duval said, "Here's news for us. News that'll probably be about your partner, Jimmy."

"If it's news of him, it's good news," said Jimmy Raeburn.

"Everything that he does is right, eh?" chuckled Rann Duval.

"Sure it is!" answered the boy.

"In spite of what I've told you about him?" said Rann Duval.

"Look," said the boy.

"Well?" asked Duval.

"Is murder worse than lying?" asked the boy.

"All right, brother. I suppose it is," said Duval.

"You're a murderer," said the boy, "so I suppose you're one of the worst liars in the world. Why should I believe anything that you say?"

A good, hearty shout of laughter came from the circle of those who listened. One man, prematurely bald-headed, with a face that slanted far forward, from forehead to chin, called out, "That's a point for you, Jimmy! Go after him, you little terrier."

Big Barry Litton gathered himself to see the cruel hand of Rann Duval strike his little prisoner; but instead, he was amazed to find that Duval was smiling at the boy.

155

The little man's chin was resting on his fist; his glance was speculating.

"You're wrong, Jimmy," said Duval. "I'm a robber and a murderer, it's true, and I can lie pretty well when the times comes for lying. But I'm afraid I can't call myself one of the best in the world. I'd like to be able to, but I can't. You know, Jim, this is an age of specialization; and although I'm a good, steady, all-round, two-handed liar, I can't say that I'm the greatest liar in the world."

"You can't help lying about Barry," said young Raeburn.

"Why can't I?" asked the other. All talk in the firelit circle stopped, and full attention was given to this dialogue.

"Because," said the boy, "you're so doggone scared of him."

"Am I?" asked Duval, with that faint and deadly smile that Litton could remember so well.

"Sure you are," said the boy. "You wouldn't dare to stand up to him—just you alone. That's one reason that you lie to me about him."

"I'll tell you one bit of truth, partner," said Duval. "The fact is that I've never gone on a man's trail in my life without warning him first!"

It amazed Litton to see that Duval condescended to argue thus with the youngster. It amazed him still more to see that Jimmy's hands were securely tied together, and that his ankles were hobbled with more cords. However, Duval was always a fellow for details such as these. He took no more chances than he had to.

"You mean that you warned Barry that you were coming after him?" asked Jimmy.

"I did," said Duval.

"You done it through a megaphone, from behind a tree, then," said Jimmy.

And the circle roared with applause, again.

"When I finally corner him," said the leader, "I'll show you his naked heart, Jim, and you'll probably find a yellow streak in it."

"When you corner him," said the boy, "you'll have to have so many helpers along with you that nobody'll ever know who really killed him.—You'll take the credit, though. When I get away from you, I'm gonna have some things to say that'll make people open their eyes."

"What makes you think you'll ever get away from me, son?" asked Duval.

"You think you can keep me?" asked the boy.

"Yes. I have an idea that I'll *have* to keep you, Jimmy. You've seen too many faces, and you know a great deal too much. I'll have to keep you, you little sparrow-hawk, until it's time for me to start some long distance riding. Then I'll have to tap you over the head, Jimmy.—Understand?"

"Yeah, you'll hate that," said Jimmy. "That's why you lemme talk now, is it? Because I'm in the death-house? Kind of privileged, ain't I?"

There was a tingle of pride in Blue Barry, as he listened to the dauntless youngster. Horror was working in him, too. He recognized the absolute finality in the tone of the great Stacey.

"You're privileged," said the leader. "Also—you've had your warning now, Jimmy—the warning I told you I always gave."

"Sure, and you always give it the same way," said the boy. "After you happen to have luck and after you've got the rope on a gent. Then you tell 'em what you're gonna do. Then you tell 'em how bright you are!—But you can't scare me, Duval."

With leering, delighted faces, the men listened and watched. A fellow at the farther side of the fire actually stood up and shaded his eyes, in order to study the features of the lad more minutely.

"Go on and tell me why you're so sure, kid?" asked the chief.

"Why," said the boy, "there ain't anything in that. It's easy! I'm not scared, because before the final minute comes, Blue Barry'll show up, and carry me off from the lot of you."

"He'll just wade right in and shoot up the lot of us?" said the leader, smiling again, in his faint way.

"He'll do that—if he has to. But he won't have to. He doesn't have to hire guns. He doesn't have to soak everything with blood. He's got brains."

"Ah! He has brains?" said Duval.

Jimmy pointed with his tied hands. "Far as you know, he may be lying back there right now—listening—with his rifle coverin' your heart, Duval!"

30. DUVAL PREPARES

"HE MAY BE OUT THERE IN THE DARK, AS YOU SAY," was all that Duval said. "Everything is a chance, Jimmy, in this little old world. But I'll tell you what I think— which is that Blue Barry Litton would rather follow the trail of the devil than mine."

"So *you* say," sneered Jimmy.

Immediately afterwards, Duval seemed to dismiss the boy's remarks. He turned to the broken-nosed man, who had been standing there silently, during a minute or more, holding the Judge's letter in his hand.

"Now what's up, Gregg?" said the little man.

"Fellow sloped up here with a message and a letter for you," said Gregg.

"Let's have 'em both," said Duval.

"Maybe you better hear the message on the side, chief?" suggested Gregg. "I don't know as you—"

"You're new with me, Gregg," said Duval. "Otherwise, you'd understand that what one of my men knows, all of them can know. I'd rather have it that way."

"The kid ain't one of your men, though," argued Gregg.

"That's true," said the leader. "But the kid's as good as a dead man. He belongs to the Dead Man Steer, already.—He's just taking a long time in the dying.—Go on and talk, Gregg."

"It's this way," said Gregg. "I get a call, and it's from the rock, all right. So I slide out and find a gent there, and I talk a little with him. He seems to be in the know, pretty deep; and he comes from Chaney. He's got a message and a letter. The message is that Holy Creek is boiling about Jimmy Raeburn."

"Let it boil. Let it boil till the pot's dry," said Rann Duval.

"It's so hot that if any of us are caught, we get the rope or even a fire," said Gregg.

"They won't do that twice to one of my men," said Duval. "You don't mean that they've tried it on Bill Parsons?"

"I dunno. There was nothing said about Bill."

"If they've touched Bill," said Rann Duval, "if they've touched him, after he was wounded when we burned out Litton . . ."

He did not raise his voice, but suddenly he stood up.

"If they've touched him, I'll catch three of 'em and hang 'em up," declared Rann Duval. And there was not the slightest doubt that he meant what he said. The very softness of his voice was the overmastering proof of his sincerity. "What else did he have to say?"

"Only that the Judge is all heated up, too. I guess if the folks in the town connect the Judge with the Jimmy Raeburn job, he'll be lynched."

"His neck's none of my business," said Rann Duval. He turned back to Jimmy. "Makes you a little proud, Jim, doesn't it?" he asked gently. "Sets you up a little, to hear that so many grown men are stewing around about one worthless kid!"

"I don't care what the crowd thinks!" answered Jimmy Raeburn. "Blue Barry is the ace up my sleeve. And when he plays, he'll take the trick. I know that."

"Will he?" said the other impatiently.

It astonished the listener hiding at the edge of the woods to hear that note of impatience in Duval's voice. Something must have departed from the great Stacey of old, Barry felt, if the talk of a boy could break down an atom of his usual strength.

Stacey snapped his fingers. "Is that the whole message?" he asked.

"That's the whole message."

"Where's the letter?"

"Here." The fold of paper was held out.

"Where's the envelope?" asked Rann Duval.

"I'm givin' it the way I got it," answered the other.

159

Duval regarded him in deadly silence for a moment, then he took the paper, unfolded and read it. Presently he refolded it, and tapped it on a forefinger.

"Gave it to you without an envelope, eh?" said he.

"That's right," said Gregg.

"Did you read it?" said Duval.

"I wouldn't believe," remarked Gregg, "that anybody that knew you would be sending you a message open, like that," said Gregg. "I thought it was just a bluff, and so I lit a match and give it a look. There wasn't no heading, and there wasn't no signature, and the letters was all printed. But I reckoned that it *might* be something that you'd want to see."

"Well, I've seen it," said Duval. He stared at the fire, crumpled the sheet, and dropped it into the flames. "I'll have a look at the messenger now," said he. "Is he back there at the rock?"

"He went off, after he give me this," said Gregg.

Duval started very perceptibly. "You mean to say that he didn't stop for a return message?"

"He said that his job was just to fetch the letter up here. That was all he was told to do, see that you got the message. He said that was all he was gonna do, but I told him he was a fool if he didn't wait. But he rode off. He was scared of stayin' too long around here, maybe.— I dunno why!" He chuckled as he said this.

"Be quiet and listen to me!" said Duval almost sharply.

Instantly Gregg was dead sober, realizing that Duval meant business.

"What was the look of this messenger?" asked Duval.

"He was about the height of me. Kind of broadish in the shoulders, an' maybe twenty-four or twenty-five years old. I noticed he kind of had a look like he would pass for a description of Barry Litton."

"Ah-h-h-h!" sighed the leader. "He had a little look of Litton about him, did he?" he demanded with dangerous quietness.

"Kind of," said Gregg.

"You mud-headed dog!" said Duval softly. "It *was* Litton!"

"Hey—look at, chief," complained Gregg. "I lighted a

160

match and looked right into his eyes. He didn't bat an eye."

"Litton could look down the throat of a cannon without blinking an eye," said the great Stacey.

"But, listen," said Gregg, still in a hurt tone of voice. "There was twenty pounds less of him than there ever was of Litton."

"Every man like Litton," said Duval, "is bigger in the memory than he ever is in fact. You stood there—you looked right into his eyes, you say? And he didn't flicker an eyelash?"

"Yeah, right straight, as hard as I could."

"They were blue eyes, I suppose?"

"Why, match light ain't the best in the world. I'd say that his eyes was kind of bluish, though. Yes, they were blue, all right."

"You stood there face to face with Blue Barry," said Duval quietly. He paused, looking down at the fire musingly.

There was a soft rustling noise, as every man around the fire, unbidden, rose to his feet; and if one gun showed, half-a-dozen blinked in the flickering light, as hand after hand drew out a pet Colt and looked to its condition.

He who lay in the covert felt what was more a stirring of grim pride than of fear, as he looked on. They knew and respected him, these men, these desperadoes, these hand-picked tools of the great Stacey.—And what a field he had to choose from!

Duval spoke again. "Men, we've got trouble ahead of us," he said. "Some of us are going to die. Barry Litton is here in the wood with us!"

A rumble of voices answered; it was like the echo of a distant thunder in the skies.

Duval went on, "I don't know where he is. He may be lying on the edge of the clearing, listening to me right now. I don't know. Anything's possible. Frankly, he's more of a man than I thought. I never dreamed that he'd dare to tackle a job like this, single-handed—or even with an army behind him. He's a brave fellow, but he never before—"

He broke off, with a curt gesture of his hand.

"You hear me, boys?" he said. "We'll go after this now. Ricky and José, take your best horses and get down

161

there just outside the woods. Keep circling the hill, slowly. If you see anything, try to break out from the woods, give the rider one hail, and then start shooting.

"Jake, come here. You and Gregg take the kid back among the trees, right on the edge of the firelight. If anybody tries to rush you, put the first bullet through the head of the brat."

"Why not do it now—and have our hands free?" said Gregg.

"It would be too much of a compliment to Litton," said Rann Duval, "that we should do that the minute we hear that he's near.—The rest of you come with me, and we'll comb the woods, from the inside out. Gregg, you understand? You've made a fool of yourself once—and once is enough!"

31. FOX AND HOUNDS

IT WOULD HAVE BEEN A BEAUTIFUL THING FOR A DIS-interested man to see the manner in which the leader organized his party. With half-a-dozen words he had the searchers organized; and presently the sound of the horses of two of the men was retreating through the woods. Jimmy was drawn back into the shadows among the trees by Jake and Gregg.

In the meantime the rest, organized as a search party, split into three sections and began to comb the woods from top to bottom, working in twisting spirals from the clearing and around the hill. Nothing escaped them. Bull's-eye lanterns with each section of the search party sent probing shafts and knives of light gliding among the branches.

Where there was any doubt a man hastily climbed up and scanned the recesses of the trees.

There was no refuge for Barry Litton amongst the boughs, therefore. The best that he could do would be to protect himself on the ground. He knew that he would be crowded rapidly to the outer edge of the woods, at the bottom of the hill, and that before many minutes. The surface they would have to cover was not great, and these searchers knew their business and wasted no time.

Once on the edge of the woods, Barry would have to get to the mare, and then break away for safety, trusting to luck that the two outer guards would not be near enough to do any effective shooting in his direction.

Even if he decided on instantaneous retreat, his way would be difficult. And if he remained, what could he do? The boy was held by two guards, with instructions to fire the first bullet through his brain.

Whatever Jake might be up to, it was plain that Gregg, having failed on one occasion to-night, would not be apt to fall short of orders on another! It was death for the boy, and death for himself, to remain.

Barry turned, and glided some fifty yards from the edge of the clearing. There he paused, with his hands against the trunk of a tree; for he recalled what Duval had said about the few remaining hours that Jimmy Raeburn had to live.

He could see the plan of the great Duval clearly from beginning to end. Jimmy Raeburn, of course, was the bait intended to be used in the capture of himself.

He, Litton, was to be drawn into the net for an instant. After his fall, the death of the boy would follow instantly, because he had, as Duval had said clearly, learned too much and seen too many outlawed faces!

But no matter what happened, it would be a dangerous—an almost impossible thing to keep the boy very long. He was hampering the movements of the outlaws; and particularly when the countryside was roused as one man against the party, Duval's men would have to be utterly free.

In a quandary, Litton remained standing, his hand resting on the rough trunk of the tree. The sweat of desperation was streaming down his face.

He turned his head. Behind him, he heard the search parties, circling. They had covered a considerable distance from the fire. Their lights glinted here and there among the trees.

He might wait until one party had passed, but that

163

would only mean that he would find the leaders of the next little group upon him immediately. There was hardly one chance in ten thousand of breaking through that flexible line in such a manner; and every segment of the line carried death in either hand!

He groaned aloud, and turned fairly about, like a man immediately at bay. A rock stood beside him, slanting well out with the slope of the hill. It was the tilt of the stone that gave him his idea, and instantly he acted upon it.

From the armpit holster beneath his left shoulder, he whipped out a Colt; and thumbing the hammer, he fired three shots into the air. Out of his throat burst a scream like that of a hunted mountain lion, or the death screech of a man in the quick, final agony.

Then, wrenching at the stone, he sent its hundred pounds of weight rolling headlong down the slope, bumping away from the trunks of the trees and crashing off the faces of other bowlders in its way. Through the smaller brush it tore its way, and bounded over the open like a live thing.

But Blue Barry had waited to see only the beginning of that descent. Then he fled straight forward with all his might, twenty sprinting yards up the slope of the hill, and dived to the ground at the base of a big tree.

Immediately he heard the answers of the searchers. They came with a rush, with shouts, until a thin, clear voice called, "Silence, everybody!—Use your ears!"

There was no more outcry. A rush of men came straight at his tree, swiftly but silently. Barry gathered himself, prepared to spring up, his gun ready, his heart set to shoot straight.

Then a flight of shadows plunged past him. Two other groups, right and left, flung by, and hurtled down the side of the hill towards the sound of that stone, which was still leaping and crashing, far ahead.

"Spread out!" sang the crisp voice of the great Duval. "Spread out—spread out! Shoot at every shadow that stirs!"

They were gone.

Almost instantly a gun rang out, and then another, another. They were shooting at every shadow, to be sure, but not at the slinking form of darkness that stole back

164

towards the clearing. Skirting the opposite side, the shadowy form moved on toward the place where it had seen the two men take the boy.

Barry could hear their voices, as he came up, and was guided almost as well as he would have been by the sheen of a light. He still heard the noise of the running men rushing down the hillside, and an occasional rattle of revolver shots.

He could distinguish Gregg, just before him, saying, "I dunno, Jake. I'd like to be in on this."

"What about the kid?"

"Put a chunk of lead through him. We can tell the chief that something seemed to come at us, so we put the kid away before we started to see what it was."

"Yeah, that would be all right—only he'd probably scalp the two of us, if he didn't feel our way!"

"Think of Litton comin' into the woods that way."

"I dunno that it was Litton. I got my doubts."

There was a sprinkling of firelight that shone through the trees, and the two men were revealed where they stood in an irregular pattern, the boy seated on the ground between them.

"Got a nice voice, your chum has," said Jake to Jimmy. "Never heard a worse holler than he made, when the lead bit into him! Yeah, like a wildcat, or a whole tribe of wildcats."

"You lie!" said Jimmy Raeburn, scornfully. "There ain't nothin' in the world that he would yell for, except to laugh at the lot of you butter-fingered saps!"

"I'd like to have the cutting out of your tongue, you brat!" said Jake, savagely.

Barry Litton rose from the brush, a gun in each hand, an open-bladed knife in the pocket of his jacket.

"Stick up your hands, and stand back to back, you cradle robbers!" he said through his teeth.

"It's Litton!" gasped Jake, and jabbed his hands straight above his head.

"Take this, then!" muttered Gregg, and fired almost as he spoke. Almost but not quite in time did he fire that shot, for the bullet from Litton's left-hand gun had beaten his own. His shot went wild, crackled through the branches of the trees, and winged into the open, as Gregg himself pitched forward on his face. He lay there on the

165

ground, gasping and groaning, clutching his desperately wounded body with both hands.

"Turn your face to that tree, Jake, and you're safe," said Litton.

Jake, with a groan as deep as that of his fallen companion, obeyed the order. Litton, with two touches of the knife, set Jimmy Raeburn free again.

"Stand quiet! Stand fast, there!" said Litton to Jake. "Back up, Jimmy—"

Barry stepped behind a tree with the lad, then glided off, speaking not a word. Jimmy stepped in his tracks, so far as the darkness permitted him to follow them.

Instantly, behind them, came a rain of bullets, crackling through the branches about them. Jake, at last, had turned. He opened up with both guns in the direction of their escape, and as he fired he screeched at the top of his lungs, "Help! Hey! Help!—Litton—Litton's here! Help! Blue Barry! Help!"

Those yells seemed to fill the wide sweep of the heavens, seemed to run like wild wolves at the heels of the fugitives as they came down the slope, working, as nearly as Litton could plot the course, toward the spot where he had left the mare.

Barry felt that a miracle had been begun—if only he could continue it through to the end—if only he could walk down the main street of the town of Holy Creek once more, with Jimmy Raeburn at his side. If that happened he would never ask for a further distinction. He would be willing to bask in the fame of this exploit forever. He would settle down to a quiet life.

The uproar of the shooting on the farther side of the hill had ceased. There was the sound of the crowd, pouring back up the hill.

Well, it would still take them some time to find Jake, and then to find the true course for the pursuit. In those few moments, much could be done.

Barry found the clustered trees and the patch of brush. He stepped through, and at his voice the mare arose from her hiding place and snorted softly. Her bridle clanked, and she shook her fine head.

"She'll carry us both," said Litton. "She'll go like the wind, too, for a little way. Jimmy, we've got to get off across that open patch. You understand? Once in the hills beyond, we'll do well enough."

He mounted, as he spoke, and reaching down his hand, he caught that of Jimmy Raeburn and helped him up with a strong swing.

Behind the saddle sat Jimmy, gasping, "They didn't get you, Barry? You're not hurt somewhere, Blue?"

"I'm sound as a fiddle," said Litton. "Hold on tight, now, Jimmy, because we're going to move." And he put the mare straight out of the wood and into the open. Time was too short to investigate how open the way might be before them.

But good fortune had deserted Barry Litton at last. As he brought the mare from the wood, two riders turned a dark promontory of the trees to his right, and hailed him with one long and pealing shout.

32. BROKEN LUCK

THEY COULD NOT BEAT DESPERATE RIDERS, WELL mounted, and Jimmy, no matter what his trust in big Blue Barry and the mare, knew perfectly well that in a short distance, if they fled, the wolves would be on their track. Others were coming, swarming down, their shouts echoing as they called to one another.

It was no plainer to the boy than to his friend. Barry Litton suddenly put spurs to the mare, and riding her with a loose rein, only his gripping knees and the sway of his body guiding her, he drove straight at the enemy, a revolver blazing from either hand.

Jimmy, crouching low and swinging out a trifle to one side, looked past Litton's side, and saw the two swing their horses toward the fugitive, then open fire.

The horse on the left suddenly spilled to the ground, throwing its rider in a long roll. He on the right, however, was as gallant a rider as Barry Litton himself. Driving home the spurs and leaning well forward, he came at the two, screeching like an Indian with every jump of his horse. His revolver was extended so that it spat fire and lead beside the very head of the straining mustang; but that horse, perfectly trained to stand under gunfire, never shrank to one side or the other.

Right before them appeared the charging outlaw; then the horse whipped past, with flying bridle reins, and with empty saddle, the stirrups tossing up wildly on either side. Somewhere on the ground lay a crumpled body; Jimmy could not make himself look back to see.

A sharp, quick voice asked, "Are you all right, Jimmy?"

"I'll be all right," said the boy. "Are you, Barry?"

"Fit as a fiddle," said Barry Litton. "More dead men for the Steer, Jimmy—more of 'em. Lots more."

The mare flew on, carrying the double burden with a wonderful lightness and ease.

"Hold tight, Jimmy!" said the rider.

Jimmy, as the mare jumped a shallow, rock-bottomed draw, was almost flung off behind. He resettled himself, securing a strong grip on Barry Litton, putting both arms around him. And as he did so, his left hand encountered a patch of warm, sticky liquid on the coat of Litton.

"Barry!" he shouted. "They've got you!"

"Don't talk like a fool!" said Litton, his voice unusually stern. "They've only nicked me, is all. I could ride a thousand miles with ten scratches like that. Hold on, Jim!"

For Jimmy, sick with the shock of his discovery, swayed and almost fell from the back of the mare, again.

They were pulling up the slope to that gap between the hills from which Litton had first looked down upon the dark hollow, and the wooded mountain that rosé in the midst of it.

The mare was brought down to a trot. To have galloped her up the ascent would have burned her out more quickly than ten miles of hard running across ordinary ground.

As she trotted along, Litton said, "Jim, it's plain that they're after us, eh?"

"They're hot after us," said Jimmy.

"There's only one way to beat 'em," said Litton. "The

mare can't carry double and run far—not at the pace she'd need to keep up in order to escape those hawks! But she can run with one."

"I'll drop off here, Barry, and hide in the rocks," said the boy. "They'll never find me."

"If they do find you," said Litton, brutally, "they'll burn you alive. You know that?"

"They'll never find me," said Jimmy, with a shudder.

"Besides," said Litton, untruthfully, "I'm not sure of the way to Holy Creek from here. Are you?"

"Yeah, sure. I know every step of the way."

"Then take the mare and run her all the way. Get to the sheriff, and start help out in this direction as fast as you can. You hear, Jim?"

"And leave you to bleed to death, here among the rocks?" cried the boy. "I'd rather be burned to death ten times running than do that, Barry!"

"Confound you!" exclaimed Barry Litton. "Are you going to argue with me, when I'm showing you a plan that'll put the rest of the gang into our hands? Do you know better than I?"

The boy was silent, hurt by the brutal bluntness of these words.

"I'm going to drop off up here," said Barry Litton. "You're going to rush for Holy Creek, and start help out here! Hear me?"

"I hear you," said the boy, grimly.

"Don't talk back, then; but do what I tell you."

"Barry, you're gonna lie out here and bleed to death!"

"By the Eternal God!" exclaimed Barry Litton. "I thought you had the makings of a man in you, but you talk like a woman. I've done a few things for you. Now I ask you to do something for me, and you stick on it.— You're afraid to ride alone—you're afraid that the mare can't beat them with her speed!"

To the very core of his soul, the boy was wounded. He said, bitterly, "I'll do what you tell me to do. I'll ride her on alone. And leave you back here—" His voice rose to a tone of anger. "You've no right to call me a woman, Barry! I ain't like a woman. I was only arguing because—"

"Then shut up now! And try to play the man, even if you don't feel like one," suggested Barry Litton. "I've had enough lip out of you, to-night. I've got a scratch, and you talk about me bleeding to death. I'm going to pull up opposite that black rock, just ahead. You be ready to switch into the saddle, then you ride like a devil for Holy Creek. The Duval boys will keep on after the mare until they see that she's carrying only one, and that one small. Then they'll turn.—

"But will they find me in the rocks? They won't, brother. They'll never find me! And while they're hunting about—d'you see?—out come the riders from Holy Creek, and curl over 'em like a wave of water! That's the way the thing will go!"

The boy gasped. Before he could speak, the mare had stopped and Litton had dismounted. As the youngster slipped into the saddle, he heard Barry Litton's voice exclaim, "Let her go!—Let her run all the way, and they'll never have a chance to tag you with a bullet, Jimmy!"

"So long!" said Jimmy, tersely, for he had been sorely stung by the other's rough language.

"Good-by, son," said Barry Litton.

He waved his hand, and the mare went off at a gallop, like a hawk on the wing. The boy was gone from sight, as the noise of the Duval gang came storming up the farther side of the hill, and Blue Barry stepped in among the rocks that covered the hilltop.

Tom Willow was on him instantly, chuckling, "You raised the devil! I could hear you strike that hill like a thunderbolt. I could hear the guns chatterin' like magpies, and I knew you were in the middle of the conversation. But—wait a minute—where's the mare?"

"Jimmy Raeburn's on the back of her, and galloping for town. And he'll bring back fifty men with guns to wipe up the Duval outfit. It's all planned, Tom—you take the mule and slither away down the far side of the hill—"

"Hold on a minute!" said Tom Willow, grimly. "I slither one way and the kid slithers another—and which way do you slither, brother?"

"Are you going to stop and argue with me, you wooden-headed fool?" exclaimed Barry Litton.

The sailor drew himself up. Instinctively he saluted. "No, sir!" he said.

With a roaring of hoofs, Duval's many riders stormed up the trail, and past.

"There they go—it's all planned," said Litton. "Take the mule and get out, now."

"Yes, sir," said Tom Willow.

He turned on his heel, made two steps, and then turned around.

"They'll be sure to come back and hunt you, sir," said he.

"I know what they'll do, and I know what *I'll* do," said Litton. "My curse is that I have to have a talking half-wit around me.—Take the mule and get out of my sight.— And stay out, will you?"

Tom Willow hesitated first on one foot and then on the other. Then he shook his head resolutely. "I won't budge a step without you," he said.

"By heaven, Willow," said the other, "you're going to drive me mad! Get out of here, and get fast!"

"I've seen you in lots of pinches," said Tom Willow, "but I never heard you talk like this before. I've heard you talk hard, but I've never heard you talk mean before. You ain't the kind to call people fools, not even if they're only Tom Willow. What's the matter with you, chief?"

"Nothing's the matter with me. I've laid a perfect plan, and you spoil it for me by hanging on when I have to be alone."

"My mind's made up more than ever," said Willow. "I ain't gonna budge a step from you—not if you take a gun on me!"

"Do you actually mean that?" cried Litton. "Do you dare to stand there—?"

"It ain't no use," said Tom Willow. "I ain't very bright, but something tells me that my place is here with you, chief."

"God bless you, Tom!" said Blue Barry. "I raised the devil back there, all right, and the devil has put a claw in me.—They've got me this time, Willow."

An inarticulate cry burst from Tom Willow. He took Litton by either arm and held him with a mighty grip.

"Where did it hit you, chief?" he asked.

"In the side, Tom," said his master. "They trimmed the wick pretty short, old boy, and I suppose the flame'll be going out in a few minutes."

"You talk clean crazy," answered the sailor. "There's

a shack back here among the rocks. We'll go there. If the crooks find us, I can keep 'em off till help comes.—The life that's in you, chief, couldn't be all let out through one bullet hole. There's the moon comin' up, to give us a light. That's luck, ain't it?—Come along this way. We got mixed up with quite a yarn, chief; but by thunder, the story is gonna have a snappy ending! I can feel it in my bones."

33. WOLF AND CAT

IT WAS THE RUDEST SORT OF LITTLE ONE-ROOM SHACK to which the sailor brought Barry Litton; and on the earthen floor of it, in the middle of the spot of moonlight which now shone through the doorless opening in the wall, Willow forced his master to lie down. His blood-soaked clothes were stripped or cut away to the waist, and that purple-welling spout was located in the right side. Willow, when he saw it, turned dizzy and sick.

When at last he found his voice, he exclaimed, "We're gonna have that little old fountain stopped in no time. Watch me work, chief!"

He ran out and came back with a hatful of fine dust; there was still some warmth from the sun of day in that heap of dust, and the sailor held a handful close against Barry Litton's side. The latter sighed with the relief that came to him at Willow's gentle touch.

"That's it," said Tom Willow. "The more pain you can let out with your breath, the better for you, and the less there'll be left inside you, chief. Ain't I heard you yourself say that, when I lay on the beach, that day yonder, with the arrow stickin' into me? Aye, you cut off the arrow head, on one side of my shoulder, and pulled out the shaft on the other; and as I began to groan, I remember you sayin' it. But this ain't nothin', Barry, this is only—"

"A ticket of leave, eh?" murmured Litton cheerfully.

"Tom, I'm comfortable now. I'm going to pull through.—
But those devils are going to get close enough to find that
the boy alone is in the saddle on the mare, and they'll
swarm back to search for me. Like a good fellow, Tom,
let me be as I am. Slip away through the rocks, now,
while there's time, and—"

"I'll fix the bandage first," said Tom Willow. "Then
we're gonna see what we see."

So, from the shirt and undershirt of his master, and by
means of pieces of his own clothes, Tom built a wide,
strong bandage, and pulled it home around a skin dress-
ing of dust, which is almost as perfect as cobwebs for clot-
ting a flow of blood.

"How's that?" he asked, as he ended the work.

"Perfect," said Barry Litton. "Give me your hand now,
Tom, and move along, will you?"

"I'll take one look around the place," answered Tom
Willow. "It might be that I can see—"

He stepped to the door as he spoke, and had his answer before his sentence was even ended. A rifle bullet
whipped through the walls of the shack, close to his head,
and as Tom ducked he heard the noise of the report.

He jumped back inside the hut.

"I might have known!" groaned Barry Litton. "I
guessed it beforehand. I might have known that I'd be the
means of pulling you down with me when I sank, Willow.—I'm sick at the thought of it, man! I'm sick at the
thought of it!"

Tom Willow pulled a revolver, and crouched at the
side of his master. "I recollect a mate of mine," said he,
"that was aboard of the *Tanterin' Castle* when she sunk,
and the skipper was old Rufus O'Cashlin. They was
sinkin', and the crew took to the boats. The last at the
side of the ship was old Rufus, and as he stood there, the
Tanterin' Castle, she give a wobble and a waver, and
sinks her stern clean under. All at once old Rufus throws
up his hands over his head and hollers, 'Pull away, boys!
Give way! There ain't room for me in a lousy little cat-
boat like that. The old *Tanterin',* she's took me safe
through every kind of storm that the seas could throw in
our faces, and, boys, we'll weather hell together, too!'

"As he says that, down goes the *Tanterin' Castle,* by
the head and the heel, in one great wallow, do you see?

There was the end of old man Rufus O'Cashlin. Well, chief, the ship that was good enough for him to live with was good enough for him to die with. And now it seems to me that the world would be damned thin drink for me, Mr. Litton, after the way that you've served it up to me, these years. If there's some dregs left in the bottom of the rum barrel, we'll take a swig of it together, sir. That's what I mean, and that's what I say!"

A sudden volley from many rifles crashed into the shack as he finished speaking.

"Lie flat, Tom!" said the wounded man.

Tom was already on his elbows. "I gotta look around a little," said Tom, "or they'll be sneakin' up to rush us, take us by surprise."

"They can't," answered the other. "They can't rush that door as fast as we can shoot 'em down! We could stack 'em there as thick as grain in the hand!"

He had turned on his side and, pillowing his head on one arm, with his right hand he touched the two revolvers which he had freshly loaded and placed in readiness.

Another salvo of rifle bullets cut through the shack walls. Tom Willow let out a roar of joyous defiance.

"They can't find us, chief!" he exclaimed. "The lay of the land is wrong for 'em, and the slope of the ground is with us. Doggone their hides, they ain't got a good chance at us, and the boy'll be leavin' Holy Creek before long!"

On the heels of these words, a terrific shock struck the shack. The whole corner of it, to their left, was torn away, and down the steep slope which the sailor had just been blessing, bounded the bowlder which had been set in motion to do that mischief.

The two glanced at one another. There was no need for words. The end was too obviously upon them.

Then, very close at hand—startlingly close—the quiet voice of the great Stacey spoke. "Hello, boys.—You both in there?"

"I'm in here alone, Stacey," said Litton.

"You've done a grand little bit of work, to-night," said Stacey. "It still has me puzzled, and I'd like to ask for a few more of the details, before we send down the bowlders and smash that shack of yours to smithereens.

There are a hundred rocks up there, in line with it. You should have thought of that, my lad."

"I should have," admitted Litton.

"We're finding some blood stains on the stones and the ground, out here. Did we nick you?"

"Just a touch, Stacey—just a touch."

"A touch that makes *you* lie flat on the ground—which by your voice is what you're doing now—" said Stacey, "is the sort of touch that ordinary men die of pretty fast. Who did the pretty trick?"

"The fellow who's lying dead in the hollow at the edge of the hill."

"Ah, did he do it?"

"Yes."

"One of my best men, Litton.—Well, 'nothing in his life became of him like his leaving of it'!—You don't mind my quotations, Barry?"

"I've always liked 'em. There's a load of poetry in you, Stacey."

"What a pity, after all," said Stacey, "that we could never work together! We could have cut the world in two, and each taken half, Barry, if we'd managed to get on together."

"We're different breeds of wolf and cat, Stacey, that's all."

"Putting me in the cat tribe, eh?"

"Yes."

"Why so, Barry?"

"Because you walk with such a soft tread, Stacey. Because you generally kill from ambush, and because there's no mercy in you."

"Three very good reasons. I love a man who has his reasons close to the tip of his tongue," said Rann Duval. "You have a lot of qualities, Barry. More qualities than any man I know of, excepting one, always."

"Meaning yourself?"

"Yes. Of course. You were always a fellow of mark, Barry. But since I saw you, you've grown a great deal. You've expanded. Your brain is richer. You're full of inventive ability. I don't mind saying that stealing Jimmy Raeburn away from me is the finest thing I've ever known about."

"That's a compliment that I appreciate," said Barry

Litton. "I know you don't throw things around like that, carelessly."

"No, it's from the heart. You were always able to put a proper value on me, Barry; and that's one of the things about you that has always charmed me. Before you die, Barry, do you mind telling me who it was that fired the shots and screeched like a dying man, back on the side of the hill, and then ran down to the bottom of it and disappeared into thin air? Don't tell me it was that clumsy fool, Tom Willow."

"Clumsy yourself, you sneakin' throat-cutter!" yelled Tom Willow.

"Ah—good!" said the outlaw. "Now I know that I have the two of you to help me fill my hands, this evening.—But it wasn't Willow on the side of the hill, was it, Barry?"

"No, not Tom Willow. I did the shooting and the yelling. And the man who ran down the side of the hill so fast was a rolling stone, Stacey. As it began to roll, I ran ahead a little distance, and threw myself down on the ground behind a tree. All of you fellows came plunging past me. Some of your people are very fast on their feet, Stacey; but as usual, they're a trifle slow in the brain. You were a trifle slow, too, Stacey."

"I was," admitted Stacey, with a perfect frankness. "I was out-maneuvered, out-tricked, and out-fought—until the very end of the battle. Then all the luck turns towards me, you see? The battle's never over, my lad, till the last shot is fired.—But on the whole, you've done a very handsome thing, Litton."

"Thanks," said the other, from the shack. "But the battle I was fighting is won, because the boy's safe, by this time."

"And as for Tom Willow? Do you count him?"

"His left hand is worth your whole gang, Stacey. I tried to send him away. I damned him, and ordered him away, when I saw that I couldn't travel very far to-night; but he preferred to stay here and sink with the ship. Can you find that sort of a man in your gang, Stacey?"

There came a soft exclamation of wonder from Stacey. Then he said, "No, I can't, Litton. It begins to appear that you've grown into such a man that I'll have to change my whole plan about you. I was going to kill you like a cornered rat, but now I see that you may be worth killing—with my own hand. There's some excellent moonlight to-night, Barry. Will you step outside and take your chances with me?"

34. WHAT SHAME DID

THE ENRAGED VOICE OF TOM WILLOW BURST OUT, "Here he's lyin' stretched out, findin' even breathin' hard —and you ask him out there to fight with ye, Stacey? —The hound that you are!"

"Are you laid out as flat as that, Barry?" asked Stacey, gently.

"If you think I am," replied Litton, "try dropping in, Stacey!"

"Think it over, my lad," said Stacey. "I don't know what makes me give you the chance, Barry. I could smash the house to bits, and you along with it, by setting some of those bowlders rolling. The boys have 'em ready to turn loose, too. But I'm giving you the chance to stand out here and take a fair shot at me. Will you do it, Barry? Are you able to stand and shoot?"

"I'm able to shoot," said Litton. "I'll soon see if I can stand!"

He pushed himself to a sitting posture.

"Stay where you are!" groaned Tom Willow. "Stay where you are, sir! It's murder for you to walk out there and face him, when you're like this."

"Isn't it murder for us to stay here like two rats in a bag, waiting to have the rocks smash us?" asked Barry Litton. Then he added to the man outside, "You've got a queer head on your shoulders, Stacey, to invite me out like this. I'd always thought you were the sort to play safe."

"It's true," said Stacey-Duval. "Only fools take chances.

177

But I'm being badly tempted, Barry—badly tempted, old boy!"

"I see," said Litton. He leaned one hand against the floor and carefully took a deep breath. A shooting pain went through his side and he turned pale. Then he added, "It's because you want to handle me a little before the finish, eh, Stacey?—With a knife would be the best, but with a gun, if you can't have anything better! Isn't that the idea?"

"That's the idea, Barry," said Stacey. "In a sense, it's a beautiful thing to think of—the bowlders smashing you to bits, and wiping you off the earth in a red smear.—Yet I'm tempted to see how you'd face me, Barry—to see how you'd be able to face me!"

"Give me your hands, here, under the armpits," said Barry Litton to Tom Willow; and the sailor, shaking his head, his face twisted with pity and horror, obediently put his hands under his master's shoulders, and helped him slowly to his feet.

There, for a moment, Litton struggled to stifle his groans, and in the excess of his agony, bowed his head against the shoulder of the sailor, put an arm around those stocky shoulders to support himself from falling.

"You ain't fit!" said Tom Willow. "You can't do it. If there's fighting, it's me that oughta go and try it.—And I'll try it, too.—Stacey, you black devil, I'm comin' out at you. Are you ready?"

"You poor fool!" said Stacey's cold voice. "Come out to be killed whenever you please. But do you think I value yours more than I value the life of a rabbit?"

"You see, Tom," murmured Litton, "it's no good.— I give you a certain pleasure, Stacey," he added, "in coming out to fight.—Will you bargain with me for it?"

"I've no idea why I should bargain," answered Stacey, outside the house. "What sort of a bargain do you want to make?"

"For Willow, here."

"Leave me out—leave me out!" said Willow. "My God, sir, would I wanta live on your blood?"

"Be still, Tom!" said the master. "I'm sick, man. Don't argue.—Stacey, if I fight you, will you let Willow go clear?"

Stacey laughed, lightly. "If you beat me, you'll both go clear, I suppose," said he.

"D'you swear to that?" asked Litton.

"You yellow dog," said Stacey, his hate and rage breaking through, "why should I swear to anything for you?—I've got you trapped. I offer you a chance to die under the open sky instead of in a corner; and yet you dare to stay there and bargain with me?"

"You've got a canteen on you, Tom," said the master. "Is there a drop of water left in it?"

"There's not a drop. You had the last of it a while ago, sir—and God forgive me!" said the sailor, in despair. "Ah, if it was the blood I could give you—"

"Old Tom Willow, you're the one with the heart," said Litton. "And I know it, well enough.—Keep your head up, man. This will soon be over, one way or another." He added, "Stacey!"

"I hear you," said Stacey.

"I'm coming out. I suppose when I show my face, you'll open up?"

"I'll give you a gentleman's chance," said Stacey. "It's not murder that I want to do on you, man. I'm going to show you that I was your master before, and that I'm your master now!—If only there was no wound on you—if you were fit and perfect—then I'd be happier."

"Strap that shoulder holster on me," said Litton to the sailor.

It was done, and the weapon hung under the pit of the left arm.

"We've been saying good-by to each other a lot of times lately," said Litton. "I suppose this is the last. If you live to see Jimmy, tell the kid that I thought of him, just before the finish, will you?"

"I'll tell him, sir," said Tom Willow. "And God's sorrow on the day that I have to say such a thing!"

"And one more—later on than the boy.—The last face I'll think of. D'you mind, Tom?"

"I hear you, sir."

"It's the girl, Tom. It was her coming the other night that made me man enough to stay for Stacey and his devils. And I'm glad that I've stayed, even if it's come to this. Will you remember that, too? To tell her that I walked out with her face in the very front of my mind?"

"Her?—The girl?" said the sailor, bewildered. "Well, sir, there's often been ladies that would of swum the seas to come to you. But it ain't by the title and the fame that a man takes a woman into his liking. I'll go to her, sir, if I live longer than you. But it ain't likely that my life'll be long. If you're gone, I'll be following."

"Likely you will," agreed Litton. "I'm only talking, in case—but I've talked too much. Help me to the door, Tom. That's it!"

Slowly, the sailor steadied him to the door; each gripped the other's hand, and then Barry Litton stepped out into the moonshine that silvered his body, bare to the waist, except for the big bandage. A rising wind threw his hair up on end, and with that clumsy bandage about his body, and the dark stains of his blood streaked upon him, he looked like a pirate out of another century.

At this picture, a wild shout that was not altogether one of hostility broke from the throats of Duval's men, who were watching from covert. It seemed to them that they had seen a miracle this night; and here was the worker of the miracle before them. He was badly hurt, but he was still a man capable of walking and shooting. They took note, too, that his gun was in its holster, and not ready, in his bare hand.

As the shout, which was prolonged, died down, the small and dapper form of the great Stacey stepped from behind a rock not ten paces away. His left hand he waved in salutation.

"Now, Barry," he said, "I can say for the first time in my life that I'm glad to see you, lad!"

"You hated me from the first, eh?" said Barry Litton.

"I hated you like poison in the air—for being a hypocrite and a sneak. It staggers me, Barry, to see you standing here in front of me, now!"

"Why," said Litton, "perhaps I could explain that, Stacey.—I'm rather surprised myself to find I have the nerve to face you to the finish. It's not for my own sake, though."

"No. Nothing ever was really for your own sake," said Stacey. "It was always to make an effect on other people. If you'd lived in the good old days, when there were soldiers of fortune, why, you would have been one of 'em. You'd have had a sword on your hip, and lace on your wrists, and manners as fine as the silks you wore. But one way or another, you're the sort that had to cut a dashing figure in the world."

"That may be true, Stacey," said Litton.

"So, even now," said Stacey, "you have to think about the way you'll figure in the eyes of the men who are watching you. It's not courage that brings you out here. It's shame, man!—Admit it, will you?"

"It's shame," agreed the other, instantly. "But I'm not thinking of the name and the fame I'll have with you and your lot, Stacey. I've learned what you're worth, and what I was worth when I was something like you."

"Tell me, my boy," said Stacey, resting his left hand against the rock beside which he stood, and smiling so that Litton could see him, in the moonlight. "Tell what we're worth."

"You're not worth the breath it would take to damn you," said Barry Litton. "If I'm shamed into trying to die like a man, it's because of two other people."

"I'd like to know their names," said Stacey, "because it seems to me you're trying to tell the truth, for the first time in your life. But I suppose it would soil their names to speak 'em, eh?"

"They're two simple youngsters," said Barry Litton. "No old name of fame about 'em, no title or that sort of thing. But they're clean-bred ones, Stacey, because the country around here breeds 'em clean and keeps 'em clean—unless man-eaters like you come in and corrupt the blood of 'em."

"Oh, damn the preludes! Let's have the names," said Stacey, impatiently. "As long as I've known you, you've always been one to moralize."

"Sam Raeburn's girl and the boy. They're in my mind now," said Litton. "Because of them, I've got to stand out here and try to die like a man."

"Because of two brats?" exclaimed Stacey. He laughed again, but more stridently than before. "Sentimental to the last!" he said. "That's what makes you such a fool. A sentimental liar to the finish."

"I'm not a liar," said Litton. "I'll tell you now—and all who can hear me—I would have run, the day you first came to see me, except that Jimmy and his sister put the

181

heart back into me. The heart of shame, man, can do almost as much as the heart of courage."

"Then fill your hand," said Stacey-Duval. "Fill your hand, and make your play!"

35. SENTIMENTAL FOOLS

NOW, IN THE LITTLE INTERVAL THAT FOLLOWED, TOM Willow stepped into the open doorway of the shack. Duval's men rose from behind the rocks that had been covering them, and their black shadows spilled down the hill, toward the place where the two men were facing each other. Eager curiosity, and something that was more than mere curiosity, forced them to show themselves in order to see clearly all that would happen in this famous moment.

There was plenty of light, for the moon was only a little past the full; one side of it seemingly had been battered roughly out of the full circle, as if it were of glowing metal that had been beaten with sledge-hammers.

Barry Litton's hand twitched, as he heard the invitation that the other had spoken. Then he shook his head. "I wouldn't have them know—the lad and the girl that I've spoken of, Stacey," said he. "I wouldn't have them know that I took advantage. We'll have it start on an even base."

"Still sentimental, eh, Litton?" sneered Stacey. "By the Lord, man, how I detest you! You don't even know.

"With you it's all stage and pretense—up to the finish. You even think you have to die on a stage—making speeches."

"That's all very well, Stacey," said Litton. "I've stopped hating you. I just want to wipe you out of the world. But I've stopped hating you, and the strangest thing in my life is that I've stopped fearing you, too."

"You lie!" said Stacey. "There's never been a time when I haven't curdled your blood."

"My voice is steadier than yours, man," said Litton, truthfully. "I've been hypnotized by you, before this. But I'm hypnotized no longer.—Are you ready? Then start the play!"

"Barker!" shouted Stacey.

"Aye?" called a voice up the hill. "Aye, chief?"

"Count as many seconds as you please, and then shoot a bullet in the air." He added, "That will be our signal, friend Barry. When he shoots, we try for one another."

"Good!" said Barry Litton. "I'm ready."

"Too bad they can't see you—all your friends," said Stacey, sneering. "A fine picture you make, man. The picture of a hero.—You dog!—And that picture will leak out, one way or another. Somehow, the world will hear about how you stood in the moonlight, with the blood running out of your body—still, dauntless, heroic. It stifles me to think of it, Litton. You've lived a lie, and you'll be famous as a lie after you're dead."

"I've never been a hired gun. And that's what you are, now," said Litton.

"Hired?" exclaimed the other.

"Aye. Hired by Chaney—and perhaps by the Morgans, too!"

"Hai!" yelled a man up the hill. "They're coming. A hundred of 'em are coming over the hills. You can pretty nigh hear the drumming of the hoofs right now! They're coming fast—every fighting man in Holy Creek, I'd say!"

"There's plenty of time," answered Stacey calmly. "They've blown their horses. We'll ride away from 'em like the wind, when we start—"

Up the hill a gun spoke loudly, and two flashes of steel answered it as Litton and Stacey drew their guns. Famous in seven lands and seven seas was the flashing draw of the great Stacey; and with it he now fairly beat young Barry Litton to the first shot—and with his bullet merely cut the air beside Barry's head.

Litton, a fraction of a second later—for the muscles were torn and dragging in his side—fired straight for the center of his opponent's body, and saw Stacey fling up his arms.

The revolver gleamed in a high arc, and dropped, even as Stacey lurched to the side and fell on his face, with sprawling arms and legs.

Neither joy nor triumph possessed Litton's heart for a single instant. It seemed to him that what had been done had happened in a dream. Some ulterior power had mastered his hand and forced it to perform this act. Stacey was down—but not, it seemed to Barry, through any great act on his part. Chance, or something else that was nameless, had done the thing.

What was real, however, was the clamor of shouting voices that broke out from the hillside. They seemed to be yelling, all of them, one thing, over and over again. "He's down! Duval's down! Get out, before they catch us!— He's down! Duval's down!"

There was a great scurrying, a clattering of small, dislodged rocks, and then one great bowlder, already up-ended, no doubt, was over-balanced, and came bounding down the hillside.

Instantly Tom Willow was beside his master. Still as though in a dream, Barry Litton saw the great mass rushing toward him, hesitating first on this side and then on that, and flinging itself high into the air as it gathered incredible momentum.

He could not move. But Tom Willow picked him up like a child and carried him to one side. The great mass of the stone struck on the very spot where he had been standing, and the next instant it crushed the shack to flinders. It carried the shattered remnants before it down the hillside, a rattling, roaring mass of confusion.

"Let me go, Tom," said Barry Litton. "Not a one of 'em stayed for poor Stacey—not a one of 'em. Let's do what we can for him, if there's anything to be done."

There was nothing to be done. They knew it the instant they turned the man on his back. His eyes were wide open and filled with understanding, but Barry's bullet had torn through the very center of his body. He spoke in a whisper, and little bubbles broke on his lips with the words, bubbles that looked black in the moonlight.

"All of them dogs," he murmured, "and every dog ran!"

With difficulty Barry Litton got down to one knee. "Stacey," he said, "it's the end of the voyage. Tell me what you want!"

"Always sentimental—to the end, eh?" whispered Stacey, with a sneer. "Give me some water."

"There's not a drop!" said Tom Willow. "But these gents that are comin', they'll have plenty in their canteens!"

Up the face of the hill, they could hear the pounding of horses being spurred against the slope.

"You win, Litton," said Stacey. "My luck ran out. Don't pat yourself on the back, though. The damned holster was wet with sweat, and my gun stuck to the leather."

"I don't pat myself on the back," said Barry Litton. "I'm done with that. You'd simply come to the end of the trip, that was all.

"Probably you would have stumbled over a pebble and broken your neck, even if I'd missed you."

"It'll please the Raeburn kid," said Stacey.

"He'll be glad that I didn't drop, all right," said Barry Litton.

"I'll tell you a fool thing," said Stacey. "The brat was in my way, and I was going to get rid of him. Still, there were a few times when he made me think, Barry."

"About what?" asked Litton. "Wait a minute, man! Don't talk just now. There may be a doctor in that lot, to pull you through—"

"Pull me through—after I've been downed? Pull me through, when the next time I fought I might think more about the chance of the gun sticking in the holster than of killing the other fellow? Or pull me through to hang?— No, be damned to it all! I'm at the end of the rope, I tell you, and I'm ready to die. I've lived my life. Mind you, Barry, I don't regret a thing.—You hear me, Willow? If either of you are men, you'll report me right. At the finish, I didn't repent; I didn't whine. Will you say that?"

"I'll say that," said Barry Litton.

"Good!" sighed Stacey. "Even I have never lied about the way that men died. Say that I damned 'em all, and that if I had my life to live over again, I'd live it exactly the same way. Will you say that?"

"I'll report it," said Litton, soberly.

"Thanks," said the dying man. "I didn't think that I'd ever live to see the time when I could thank you, Barry— and mean it.

"But now I'll add another thing. As long as I had to die, it's better to die from a bullet out of your gun than

185

from a shot of some lucky fool of a bounder. The kid, though—"

His voice failed, and a horrible bubbling sound filled up his throat.

"He's gone," said Tom Willow.

"You lie," said Stacey distinctly, the next moment. "I'll live to finish what I want to say. It's a confession, Barry, that I've been a sentimental fool, like you.

"I used to think, when I was in camp with Jimmy Raeburn, that if things went another way with me, I'd marry, one of these days. And if I had done that I'd have wanted to have a saucy brat like that for a son."

"Aye, Stacey," said Barry Litton gently, "and I've had the same idea."

"You would have it," said Stacey. "A sentimental fool like you—you would have it, of course! If you were a man like—"

His voice went out; his head fell back. They knew that he was dead, even before they listened for the beat of the heart.

And the thunder of the riders poured up the hill and broke about them.

36. SETTLING DOWN

THE RIDERS CAME WITH A RUSH, AND WOULD HAVE gathered in pools around the dead man and the figures of big Blue Barry and Tom Willow. But the sheriff was there, and it was he who carried the best riders off on the trail of Duval's men.

There was one rider who remained, however, and that was little Jimmy Raeburn, who came with a leap from his own small mustang. Then he winced away from the sight of his hero, half naked and covered with his own blood.

Blue Barry, needing support, put his hand on the shoulder of that small form.

"Everything's finished, Jimmy," he said. "Sit down with me, and talk, and don't stop." He staggered a step or two, sat down, then lay down, and remained there, with his arms cast wide.

Jimmy Raeburn did not cry for help. He did not need to. Those who had followed the sheriff had been only those whose horses were good enough and fresh enough for a fast run. The others halted at the scene of the fight, and they grouped themselves compactly around the fallen man, to do what they could.

Tom Willow took charge. He sent two men galloping for water. Others assisted him in taking off the old bandage and its great handful of clotted blood and dust. Still others gave their clothes and their help in arranging a second bandage.

Tom Willow placed Jimmy Raeburn close at the side of the wounded man.

"If he cracks his eyes open pretty soon," said Tom, "you're the mug that he'll wanta see, kid."

Jimmy Raeburn looked up proudly, with tears pouring down his face. "God wouldn't let nothin' happen, Tom, would he?" asked Jimmy.

"God? God wouldn't be such a fool," said Tom Willow, soberly.

For his own part, he went to the still body of the fallen man, Rann Duval—the man called Stacey in another part of the world. Reaching into the dead man's pockets, Tom found at last a certain pigskin wallet which was stuffed with greenbacks of a large denomination. These the sailor scattered scornfully on the ground. Attentive, watching eyes saw them fall, and careful hands gathered them up.

But the things that Tom Willow found which interested him were certain brief notes. Some were signed by the celebrated Judge Chaney. Others were signed by the head of the Morgan clan. Their purport was exceedingly clear.

Tom Willow stood up before the crowd and read them out. Faint, but deep-throated angry murmurs greeted the reading.

The receipt of certain sums of money was acknowledged, but what was clearest of all was that Stacey had been playing off the Morgans against the Chaneys. He

187

had promised the Dead Man Steer to both factions. He would deliver it, if possible, to the highest bidder.

But now the outlaw was dead, and his plots were dead with him. There remained the Chaneys and the Morgans—and Blue Barry Litton.

Tom Willow spoke a brief sentence, "They'd oughta hang! I dunno that Barry'll live through it; but anyway, the Chaneys and the Morgans, they'd oughta hang!"

Yet when certain bands of masked men rode up to the Morgan and Chaney houses, they found that the game they wanted had disappeared. They had disappeared for good, as far as that part of the world was concerned. The Morgans and the Chaneys had simply melted out of that section of the range.

The town took little notice, apparently. If sufficed that the leaders had left immediately, and that the gangs of hired gunmen had dispersed.

Two things happened on the following day. The first was that Sheriff Dick Wilson rode into the town, bringing with him five members of the fugitive Duval gang. The second was that Barry Litton was carried up through the street of the town of Holy Creek on a hand litter borne by the most prominent citizens of the town. The wounded man was brought to the house of Samuel Raeburn. Young Jimmy Raeburn and his sister Lou gave succinct directions as to what was to be done for him.

Shortly afterward, a great noise broke out. It was a noise of groaning and of cheering, and the center of it was the form of a big, lazy, ambling Texas steer. On its flank was branded the grotesque and horrible sign of a skull with crossbones beneath it.

The animal was being led down the main street of the town. And wherever it appeared, men threw up their hands and shouted.

For it was the end of the reign of the Dead Man Steer. Whatever else happened, no more men would die because they claimed ownership of the steer. Ownership had passed, without further dispute, into the hands of the man who had fought to keep it for the hands of the law—Barry Litton.

There was another little matter which caused the town of Holy Creek to sleep on arms for some days. That was the action of the Governor of the State, who threatened to call out the militia to enforce the arrest of the notorious criminal, Barry Litton. The legislature promptly passed a vote of censure, and the Governor straightway discovered some "new" evidence. Presently a "pardon" appeared for Barry Litton.

As for the states and the countries in which that pardon was not current coin of the realm, at least they were too prudent to send officers to Holy Creek with warrants for arrest.

And Barry Litton himself?

Everything happened as any man of imagination could have foreseen. The tyrant in the business, from first to last, was Jimmy Raeburn himself. He did not understand how a fellow like Barry Litton could throw himself away on a girl like Lou. Neither did the rest of Holy Creek, for that matter. She had always been the most popular girl in the town, to be sure; but she had no right to shine at the side of such a hero as Barry Litton.

On the day when it was announced that Barry was out of danger, the townsmen caught up the doctor, and carried him up and down the main street on their shoulders, shouting and whooping. His fame and his fortune were made. As long as he lived, he would be known as the man who saved Barry Litton's life. He was a made man for life.

Lou Raeburn talked all this over with the patient, on an evening in the early summer, as he lay propped in his bed.

"You know, Barry," she said, "we ought to look forward a little bit. What are your plans?"

"To marry you, young woman," said he.

"Oh, I know about that," she said, impatiently. "But afterward?"

"To live happily ever after," said he.

She permitted herself the thinnest of smiles.

"But *where* are we going to be happy? How are you going to invest your money and your time, Barry?" she insisted.

"My money?" said he. "If I knew just which people had lost it, I'd give it back to 'em, of course. Since I can't tell that—because they're scattered so far apart, I'm going to give it to charity. I'll ask Jimmy's advice about that."

"But what will you do without the money, Barry?"

189

"I'm going to work."

"At what?"

"What do you suppose?"

"I don't know," said she. "But I'll follow, Barry, no matter what or where it is."

"It'll simply mean waiting," said he, "because I'm settling down here in Holy Creek. It may not be the biggest nor the brightest town in the world, but it's my town."

"And mine," said she. "But what will you do?"

"Ride range, punch cattle," said he. "There are a lot of things about cows that I don't know, but I'm going to start in learning."

She closed her eyes, but her smile was happy. "And all the other countries, and all the other men and women, Barry?" she said. "And everybody who knows you?"

"They don't count," he told her. "And nobody really knows me—except you and Jim."

"Bother!" said she. "How could a boy like Jimmy—?"

"Hey, Jim!" shouted big Blue Barry.

"What's the matter, Barry?" called Jimmy.

"Come in here. Your sister's running you down."

The boy's voice came back to them. "You go in there and dress 'em both down, Tom," said Jimmy Raeburn. "They're kind of getting out of hand."